Also by Patty Froese Ntihemuka:

Martha and Mary
Mary: Call Me Blessed
The Woman at the Well

The Hyacinth Chronicles:
Hyacinth Doesn't Go to Jail
Hyacinth Doesn't Grow Up

To order, call
1-800-765-6955.

Visit us at
www.AutumnHousePublishing.com
for information on other Autumn House® products.

PATTY FROESE NTIHEMUKA

ZACCHAEUS

WHEN GOD Stopped By

Autumn
House® Publishing
www.autumnhousepublishing.com
A Division of **REVIEW AND HERALD®** PUBLISHING
Since 1861

Published by Autumn House® Publishing, a division of Review and Herald® Publishing, Hagerstown, MD 21741-1119

Autumn House® titles may be purchased in bulk for educational, business, fund-raising, or sales promotional use. For information, please e-mail SpecialMarkets@reviewandherald.com.

Autumn House® Publishing publishes biblically based materials for spiritual, physical, and mental growth and Christian discipleship.

Some of the details and dialogue in this book expand on the biblical story but are based on what is currently known about the times and the culture of the biblical world.

The author assumes full responsibility for the accuracy of all facts and quotations as cited in this book.

This book was
Edited by Penny Estes Wheeler
Cover designed by Ron J. Pride
Cover photo by Trent Truman
Typeset: 12/14 Bembo

PRINTED IN U.S.A.

15 14 13 12 11   5 4 3 2 1

Library of Congress Cataloging-in-Publication Data
Ntihemuka, Patty Froese.
    Zacchaeus : when God stopped by / Patty Froese Ntihemuka.
        p. cm.
    1. Zacchaeus (Biblical figure)—Fiction. 2. Bible. N.T.—History of Biblical events—Fiction. I. Title.
    PR9199.4.N825Z33 2010
    813'.6—dc22

                                            2010017768

ISBN 978-0-8127-0503-4

Dedication

To my husband and our beautiful son.

They are my everything.

Contents

CHAPTER 1

OSHRI

Tzofit did not hate him. While she had never liked her husband, and that had been no secret to Yericho at large, she was quite certain that she did not hate him. Hate would be a sin. In fact, as she stood in the courtyard next to her cooking fire, the smoke stinging her eyes as she peered into the murky, bubbling pot, she could think of several things that she liked about him.

First of all, Oshri did not smell. He washed himself and did not acquire that rank stench some men seemed to build up over time, following them around like a loyal goat. Yes, she liked that. He also provided well for her. She couldn't complain about that. His father was wealthy and they were quite well off. Thirdly, he tended to leave her alone. At least in recent years. There had been a time when she'd begged God that her husband would spend more time out of the house, and God had answered that prayer. He was away much of the time. She liked that most of all.

"Watch yourself!" Tzofit barked. Her maid froze, blushed, and stammered something unintelligible. Tzofit held the girl's eye in a silent stare before muttering, "Idiot!" under her breath and turning back to the stew simmering over the fire. It wasn't like the meal mattered much anyhow. There were no guests and her mother-in-law and father-in-law were well used to her cooking. Her husband wasn't going to be eating . . . not in the state he was in. The man was incredibly ill. It kept him home, which was irritating, but it also meant he couldn't sneak up on her or put up much argument. There were worse things than a sick husband.

Tzofit dipped the spoon into the bubbling, spattering pot and blew on it tentatively before sucking some of the hot stew between her teeth. It wasn't her best. But then, Tzofit had never been much of a cook. She could adequately mix ingredients, but that special something extra that made a meal sumptuous was always missing. And there was normally too much salt.

"Go fetch the water," Tzofit snapped. She directed the words in front of her, knowing that her maid was behind her. She heard the girl stop the grinding she was doing and push herself to her feet. She did not turn to see her leave. She got satisfaction from ordering the maid about. The girl was an idiot, anyway, and wouldn't know her foot from a broom if not given direct orders.

The morning was warm, and the sun soaked into her shoulders and back, toasting her comfortably. Her veil lay down around her shoulders and her sleeves were tied back to leave her arms free. The waves of heat from the fire pushed against her robes, filtering through the fabric to her legs beneath. She sighed softly to herself, listening to the sound of the goat munching rhythmically on some grass. It gave a soft "meh" sound, and she glanced at the little milk goat, its large eyes lazily watching her by the cooking fire.

"Tzofit?"

She turned to see her mother-in-law, her veil down around her shoulders exposing her gray streaked hair she'd pulled back in a bun. The woman stood in the doorway. The curtain hanging there to keep the dust outside had caught over her shoulder.

"Yes?" Tzofit swung her gaze back to the pot.

"Don't you care how he is?"

"Of course," she replied. "How is he?"

The older woman was silent. So this was how it would be. Tzofit suppressed a small smile. She and her mother-in-law played these games often. Tzofit refused to look back, and let the silence stretch.

"A good wife would be at his side!" her mother-in-law said in an icy tone.

"You were there," Tzofit said. "There was no room. Besides, someone had to cook."

"He's my boy," she said, her voice quavering. "I gave birth to him. I nursed him."

"Perhaps I will go check on my dear husband," Tzofit murmured, putting a sweet smile on her face. "If you would be willing to see to the stew, of course."

As Tzofit walked from the courtyard, she heard her mother-in-law sipping noisily from the long-handled spoon.

"Oh, for the love of—" she heard the gasp.

The stew wasn't *that* bad! Tzofit resisted the urge to say something back and kept on walking, her chin held high. If her mother-in-law hated her cooking so much, she should see to the cooking herself. Her father had liked her stew. He had called her a lovely cook and pinched her cheek. She'd been barely 12 then, of course, and perhaps her father had hoped that her cooking would improve with time. But she still clung to his compliments.

"What a wife you'll make!" he'd exclaimed. "Such a wonderful cook and such a pretty face."

And as if to show his sincerity in the words, he married her off the next year. Oshri was the lucky man, and she was deposited into her mother-in-law's kitchen. She had never heard a compliment since.

The bedroom that Tzofit shared with Oshri was on the main level off the living area. His parents slept upstairs in the room above, and the servants slept on mats in a covered area of the courtyard. It gave them relative privacy. The room now smelled of illness with the faint aroma of vomit hovering in the air like a cloud of gnats. She rubbed her hands over her eyes, sighed, then pushed the door open.

Oshri lay on top of a low bed with a mattress stuffed with straw, his eyes shut. He wasn't sleeping, though. She could tell by the way he was breathing. The striped blanket that had covered him was pushed onto the floor at the end of the bed, and a lighter covering had twisted around his legs.

"Mother?" he whispered.

"No," Tzofit said.

He opened his eyes and squinted against the light. He looked feverish and worn. He looked at her and sighed, closing his eyes again. Tzofit stood awkwardly in the doorway. She was not a comfort to him. She knew it. He much preferred his mother's presence, but then he always had. Why he'd bothered taking a wife was beyond her.

"Would you like some water?" she asked after a few moments of listening to him breathe.

"Send Mother," he sighed. "She doesn't spill it on me."

"She is busy in the kitchen," Tzofit said giving him a tight smile. She filled an earthen cup from a jug on a table nearby and squatted next to his bed, then slid her arm under his neck and tried to lift him.

"You'll have to at least try, man," she muttered, and he struggled to help her raise him enough to drink. His back felt shockingly bony and his skin was hot to the touch. He was much more ill than she'd thought.

He slurped back the water, but as soon as it was down, he moaned, turned his head to the side, and brought it back up onto her lap. Tzofit sat still for a moment, feeling the vomit soaking through her robe and tunic to her legs beneath. The stench filled her nose. It was all she could do to keep from gagging.

"Can you take a small sip?" she asked after a moment. "Not a big gulp, just a small sip?"

He shook his head, turning away. It didn't look good. She pulled the soiled cloth away from her plump legs and prepared to rise, grimacing at the feeling of something wet running down her leg.

"Tzofit," he said softly.

"Yes, husband," she replied. She looked down into his face, noting how his black beard grew all the way up past his cheekbones, and how his eyebrows came together over his nose so that they blended together in a single line. She felt a wave of tenderness. It was hard not to feel something for someone so helpless. "Is there something that might help you feel better?" she asked with a low tone.

"Send my mother, Tzofit," he sighed. "I need her."

Tzofit rose with as much dignity as she could muster, holding the rank fabric away from her body. She took a deep breath through her nose, regretting the habitual sniff as soon as she smelled the vomit once more.

"If you don't drink something, Oshri, you will die," she said matter-of-factly. "This is not the time to play games."

And she turned to leave the room. As she reached the door she turned back, a cold smile coming to her lips. "You should know, Oshri, that your mother is busy in the kitchen now," she said. "I will not disturb her."

With that paltry victory, she left the room.

Tzofit's servant lowered the large earthenware pot to the ground and wiped a stray hair from her eyes. There were other women in front of her waiting for their turn at the well. It would not be long, but she wished it would take an eternity . . . anything to keep her away from her mistress for a few minutes longer. Her shoulders ached, as did her back.

She hated Tzofit. She hated her so much that she dreamed about it. She longed to be able to say something . . . to put into words her loathing and distain. But to do so would be dangerous in the extreme. If she didn't want to be beaten within an inch of her life, her mouth needed to stay solidly shut.

Idiot. Simpleton. Your mother's mistake. The words swirled around in her mind like garbage in a gutter. She was no simpleton. She may not know how to act around her betters, but she was anything but simple. She knew everything that happened in that home. She knew that Tzofit's husband was afraid of his icy wife. She knew that he avoided contact with her as much as possible, staying out very late "on business," if that was what the higher classes were calling it these days. She knew that Oshri preferred his mother to his wife, and given the choice between time alone with either one of them, his mother would win the contest every time. She knew that Tzofit, for all her sharp words and anger, was not a loved woman.

She crossed her arms over her chest and stared gloomily into the empty pot.

The servant was not loved, either.

Zacchaeus knocked on the dense wooden door once, hammering hard with the heel of his fist, then looked away, waiting for the servant to open for him. He could hear the scrape of the peek-door opening, but still he refused to look. Then the latch opened and he looked up into the passive face of the serving girl. She was pretty, in that sturdy, low-class kind of way. She had a large nose, but expressive, moist eyes. Her lips were an attractive pout in a wide face.

"Where is your master?" Zacchaeus asked.

"Your father has not returned yet, sir," she said.

"And my brother?"

"He is ill, sir," the girl said, looking down on him with a practiced look of humility. "He is in his sleeping quarters."

"Still?" Zacchaeus asked, squinting against the dim light. "Is he any better?"

"I'm not sure, sir," she said softly. "His wife would know. She is in the courtyard, sir."

Zacchaeus rolled his eyes. He had no use for Tzofit.

"Tell my mother I'm here," he said, watching her bob in a quick curtsy before slipping away in soft sandaled feet. He looked after her for a moment, his eyes narrowed in thought. Then he turned and walked briskly back toward his brother's sleeping quarters, his short legs making the brisk walk less than brisk if you compared it to the walk of another man. Or even to that slave girl. He hated looking up at the household help. It never felt right to look up at a servant. He paused at the door to the room, listening for the sound of another person inside.

"Oshri?" Zacchaeus called softly.

He heard a low moan within. Pushing open the curtain, he felt the odor hit him like a wall. It was the combination of sweat, vomit, and urine, strong enough to make his eyes water momentarily. He swallowed hard and looked around his brother's room. The bed, big enough for two people, was pushed against the wall. A pile of soiled linen lay bunched in one corner waiting to be removed. A window let a shaft of afternoon light into the room, falling across the swept tiled floor and caressing a plastered wall like a woman's tentative touch. His brother lay on the bed and he turned his head, squinting blearily at him.

"Zach?" he said, his voice a hoarse whisper.

"You look like a chariot accident," Zacchaeus said. An attempt at humor.

"You look . . . like a lion's feast," Oshri said, laughing breathlessly.

Zacchaeus kicked a tunic across the floor toward the general pile, then squatted down next to the bed. His robe fell in heavy folds over his broad shoulders and wide chest and rested on the floor in expensive folds. Zacchaeus scratched at his closely cropped beard and pressed his lips together thoughtfully.

"Seriously, brother," Zacchaeus said. "You don't look good."

"And you look . . . two feet too short," Oshri gasped.

Zacchaeus belted out a laugh, but resisted punching his brother in the side the way he normally did. Oshri looked fragile. Pale. Brittle. Zacchaeus felt a finger of worry move through his stomach.

"I've never been tall," Zacchaeus said. "But I could always lift more than you, you runt."

"Because you don't have far to lift," Oshri replied, his lips stretching into a grin.

"Where is Mother?" Zacchaeus asked, his tone softer. "Why are you here all alone?"

"The women are . . . cooking," Oshri replied, his voice a hoarse whisper. "My . . . wife just left."

Zacchaeus made a face.

"I saw that," Oshri said.

"I was thinking of Tzofit's cooking," Zacchaeus replied. "Don't blame me for not being able to forget, brother."

Oshri made a face back and chuckled. "Everything disagrees lately. Can't keep anything down."

Zacchaeus looked around and spotted a jug of water close by.

"Should I pour some water for you?"

Oshri shook his head. He made a small gesture with his hand to indicate the water did not stay down, either. Zacchaeus nodded and looked down at his own square hands. They were soft—hands that did not do hard labor. His were hands that counted coins. They were hands that were awkward caring for sick people.

"Remember that old tree we used to climb?" Oshri asked. His voice seemed a far away whisper.

"The sycamore?"

"We used to watch the girls . . . going to fetch water," Oshri said with a hoarse chuckle.

Zacchaeus gave a wry laugh. "The only time I could see over anyone's head."

"I keep dreaming of that tree."

"What of it?"

"In my dream I'm watching the girls go for water," Oshri said quietly. "It's . . . nice . . ."

Zacchaeus nodded. He understood. There was freedom in being a boy. The freedom to dream. To hope and wish. Freedom that evaporated upon reaching manhood. Freedom that did not exist in the face of duty to one's family.

"I remember how pretty the tanner's daughter was," Zacchaeus said.

Oshri nodded silently.

"Better looking than the high class girls," Zacchaeus said. "I remember calling down to her from that tree, telling her she was a dove among crows."

Oshri let out a wheezing laugh.

"Laugh now, brother, but her words stung," Zacchaeus said peevishly.

"Called you . . . a . . . sinful . . . ugly . . . toad . . ." Oshri said between breaths. He sighed. "Good with . . . words, that one."

"You had a crush on her," Zacchaeus retorted in good humor. "On the tanner's daughter, of all the girls to choose!"

"Didn't marry her," Oshri pointed out, frowning at the teasing.

"No, you didn't." Zacchaeus let the joke drop.

Both men were silent. Oshri breathed heavily, obviously tired from the exertion of talking. Zacchaeus looked down at his hands again, looking at his stubby fingers, his nails trimmed and buffed. They were both thinking of the woman Oshri did marry. Tzofit. Zacchaeus felt a boyish nervousness even thinking about the sharp-tongued shrew.

"Women!" Zacchaeus said, waving his hand dismissively.

"Women," Oshri echoed, but his voice was less certain. He looked toward the door.

"Where's Mother?" he asked.

Zacchaeus's eyes followed Oshri's glance toward the door. He had no intention of wandering into the women's domain. If it were only his mother he wouldn't mind, but his sister-in-law intimidated him.

"Did you want some water?" Zacchaeus asked instead.

"No."

"You should have some, brother," he said. He pushed himself to his feet and went to the table, reaching up and pouring an earthen cup of sun-warmed water. He returned to his brother's bed and put one strong arm under his shoulders and hoisted him up.

"No . . ."

"Drink it, Oshri." It was a command. "You need water. You know it."

Oshri took a thirsty slurp of the water, swallowed, made a face, and the water came up with bile onto the blanket beside him. Zacchaeus sat motionless, the rank smell of vomit rising up to him like steam from burnt stew.

"I'll get Mother," he said after a moment.

He didn't know what else to do.

CHAPTER 2

CROSSING THE RIVER

The steady stamp of the soldier's feet was a comforting sound to Gaius Markus Africanus. The creak of the leather joints in armor, the smell of oiled cuirasses glinting in the afternoon light, and the sight of his steel-eyed squadron marching in formation behind his chariot, their armor clattering with each step, warmed his heart in the same way the aroma of fish sauce and fresh bread did. The smell of sweaty padding underneath the metal armor, the rub of his helmet on the back of his head, the feeling of the leather reins biting into his palms as his horses strained forward—all reminded him that he was part of something much larger than himself. He was part of the army, the Roman army that could never lose.

Standing in full armor did something to a man. It steeled him. It strengthened him beyond his muscles and sinews into something tougher and more fearless. He ceased to be a man, a Roman, a citizen, and became a soldier. Or in his case, a centurion—leader of 84 soldiers, not all of whom were stationed with him this day. Standing in full armor transformed a man into something greater than he could ever be without the muscled cuirass, the sword, the short spear, the belts, buckles, and padding that protected his flesh from the constant rub of metal and hard leather. There was something about the smell—the mixture of sweat, oiled leather, and metal polish—that somehow lifted him above the stink of Yericho's streets.

A soldier was a man trained to fight. He was trained to fight en mass with his unit, and he was trained to fight alone. Looking at any man, he saw only the weak points—the soft flesh of the belly, the knees vulnerable to the right amount of side pressure, the bobbing Adam's apple so easily crushed. He saw every man in terms of his vulnerabilities. He saw every man as a certain number of steps before he was a corpse. This made a soldier dangerous.

"Wait outside!" Gaius ordered. The soldiers slammed their fists into their cuirasses in salute and took their positions outside the door of the tax collector. They were trained to watch for anything suspicious, and Gaius knew he could trust them to do their jobs precisely.

He liked the house. It was well built, beautifully decorated in that dark, cozy Jewish manner. It was large. There was the main house with an enclosed courtyard that extended out the back, complete with a pool of water pumped in from the aqueducts, thanks to Rome. There was an upper level that was more than a small room. It had three windows facing the road, and he could see the fine quality of the multi-colored billowing fabric that covered them. The Jewish decorating style left much to be desired, in Gaius' opinion, but he had to admit that Zacchaeus had excellent taste.

He pounded on the door with three hard thumps then stepped back so that Zacchaeus' security guard could see him, face immobile and muscles taut. The door swung open, and the big, burly man gave him a small nod, allowing him entrance.

"Where is the tax collector?" Gaius asked bluntly. His eyes swung around, taking in the entryway. Carpets displaying intricate weaving hung on the walls. From Persia, no doubt, judging from the style. A small serving girl appeared in a white shift belted at the waist. She had a round face and eyes that betrayed nothing. She dropped to one knee in front of him.

"Tell your master I am here," Gaius said. The girl knew who he was. He saw her every visit, although she never let recognition light up her eyes. Stubborn one, that girl. But a good servant.

Without a word, the girl rose and walked noiselessly away. A moment later, his host appeared, a smile on his face.

"Come inside, come inside," Zacchaeus said. He threw his arms wide in a gesture of welcome. He was a short man. Short, actually, was too soft of a word. He was a hand span taller than the dwarves he had seen entertaining at Herod's palace. Zacchaeus' shoulders came up to Gaius' belt, but those shoulders were strong and broad. For all of his diminutive stature, the tax collector was well built. Keeping one's body in shape mattered to a Roman, and Zacchaeus did an admirable job. He had the Jewish beard, trimmed neatly, the dark complexion, and the large nose, but his clothing betrayed a sense of style beyond his heritage. Wealth could be a grand tutor.

"Come, I am just eating," Zacchaeus said, beckoning. "My cook has outdone herself today. You must come and refresh yourself."

Gaius shook his head, a smile twitching at the corners of his lips. He had worked in this region for three years now, and had grown to genuinely like the chief tax collector of Yericho.

"I have orders to deliver the taxes," Gaius said, apology tingeing his tone.

"Of course," Zacchaeus nodded. "Then we will talk business. But first you must try these delectable leeks."

Zacchaeus turned to beckon to a servant, and when he did, Gaius saw the dark circles under the smaller man's eyes. The whites looked bloodshot, and Gaius wondered what had happened. The perfect host, Zacchaeus would never mention it.

"My friend," he said, lowering his voice. "What has happened in your home?"

Zacchaeus looked back, his eyes going from questioning to relief.

"My brother is ill," he said simply.

"Very ill, I take it," Gaius replied.

"I've told you of him many times," Zacchaeus said. "He was the imp who would play tricks on me as a boy." He shook his head, a reminiscing smile coming to his lips.

"He is still on this side of the river?" Gaius asked delicately.

"For now," Zacchaeus nodded. "For now, Elohim willing."

Gaius pursed his lips and crossed his arms over his cuirass, the metal at the edges pressing into his biceps. He looked down at his sandaled feet, the crisscrossed and steel studded leather covered in dust from the streets.

"It's the wife," Zacchaeus said suddenly, shaking a finger at Gaius meaningfully.

"Your brother's wife?"

"She's a hideous shrew, that woman!" Zacchaeus said. "Tongue as sharp as a razor and skin like a snake. She's vile, I tell you!"

"You think she's poisoned him?"

Zacchaeus eyes lit up for a moment, then the light died.

"No," he said, shaking his head. "But her bedside manner is severely lacking, man. What good is a wife unless she can care for you when you are sick? Her heart is as small and hard as a pebble. I don't think a tear has ever moistened the skin of that cheek."

Zacchaeus walked slowly toward his office, a small room with no windows at the back of the house before the courtyard. Inside, oil lamps flickered, illuminating the small room with a warm glow that seemed more like night than midday. Gaius' instinct as a soldier suddenly piqued, and he kept an eye on the open doorway leading to the courtyard. A perfect ambush spot, if one had a motive. He moved the curtain with the butt of his spear and saw nothing. He turned his attention back to the small Judean in front of him.

"Dreadful," Zacchaeus was saying. "Truly, deeply loathsome."

"There is no love lost between yourself and your sister-in-law, I take it," Gaius said with a chuckle, his eyes scanning the office in a quick, professional survey.

"How can a woman resist this?" Zacchaeus asked with a grin, spreading his arms wide to display the perfect cut and drapery of his robe. "But on my part, my friend, there is no wasted love, you are right."

He turned back to the room and pushed his desk aside. Then he bent and flipped back a carpet, exposing a locked wooden chest imbedded in the tiled floor. Taking a key from the belt under his robes, he opened the box and pulled out a leather bag bulging with coin. He deposited the bag on the desktop with a clatter, then leaned down to return his hiding place to its proper state.

"It's all here, according to the reports," Zacchaeus said, turning suddenly businesslike. He tugged at the leather thong that tied it shut and poured the contents onto the desk. His fingers moved nimbly over the coins, collecting like denominations together into one handful and dropping them into perfectly stacked piles.

"Ten, ten, ten . . ." he said as he stacked. "And five, and six, and seven."

He moved to the smaller coins, expertly arranging them for quick counting. Gaius looked down at the report in his hand, his eyes flickering back up to the money as Zacchaeus counted. It was a large sum. Zacchaeus was good at what he did, and honest. Well, as honest as Rome cared for him to be. He didn't swindle Mother Rome, and that was as far as Gaius cared to worry.

"It's correct," Gaius said, and then stepped forward to put the coins back in the leather bag as was protocol. No matter how trusted the tax collector, the centurion handled the money after the counting. If a coin or two was palmed away, it was the centurion who answered for the loss. Gaius had no intention of having any missing money on his report. He pulled the thong tight and weighed the bag thoughtfully in his hand before placing it in a box he had brought with him and locking it.

"A brother is the closest a man can have," Gaius said quietly.

"Yes," Zacchaeus agreed. "Closer than a woman."

Gaius looked into the face of the shorter man and saw the dark, sad eyes, the deepened lines around his mouth, despite the customary smile.

"Well!" Gaius said with a brisk nod.

"Till next time," Zacchaeus said and put one hand over his heart and bent his head, a softer version of the Roman salute. "Find some excuse for an extended visit, friend. The food in my home is superb."

Gaius did not doubt it. But Romans did not socialize with Judeans. Social expectations would not allow for it. He wondered as he walked back out into the blinding daylight if he were the tax collector's only regular visitor.

Benyamin rubbed the back of his neck where a horsefly had bitten him. He resisted the urge to scratch, knowing it would only sting more. He mentally cursed the insect, wishing a hideous death on it. Something more painful than a quick, simple squashing. His skin was dry from the dusty, windy day, and he spat some grit from between his teeth then smoothed his long beard with one hand, feeling the springy fullness of it melt into the wispy ends at chest level.

His attention was not on the fly, however. He was watching the wealthy home of one of the chief tax collectors, a squadron of Roman foot soldiers guarding the door. Their gazes moved over him, immediately dismissing him as unimportant. This was not the first time he was dismissed so quickly. It happened often. Benyamin was not an imposing man. Nor was he an impressive man. But he was a devoted man—devoted to the law of God . . . devoted to Israel. Devotion was much more dangerous than the occupiers realized.

Disgusting pig! He felt bile rising in his throat at the very sight of the rich man's house. Zacchaeus was wealthy off the backs of his neighbors. He'd sold his soul to Rome, groveling at their feet and squeezing the very bread from the mouths of Jewish children. He represented all that was loathsome and ugly . . . the people of God who had turned from the true worship of Adonai and joined the detestable cringing before idols. He spat in the dust, his lips twisting in disgust. A man like that deserved stoning. A man like that would have been stoned without further thought in the good old days . . . the days when Elohim led His people by a pillar of cloud and fire. This was what had become of Yudah . . . this . . .

Benyamin turned his eyes away as the door opened and the centurion exited, followed by the hideous little sinner. His mother must have the vilest of sins hidden under her veil to have birthed such a freakish spawn. Benyamin looked sideways at the centurion and the fawning little tax collector. It was midday. Obviously the taxes had been collected by Rome, and they would be brought to the civic center of Yericho. He eyed the locked box that was being loaded into the chariot.

That box held the hard earned coin of his people. That box held the hopes and dreams of a conquered nation. It held the possibility of full bellies, the chance at a proper cloak for too many of the people of Yericho. They were taxed to death. What Rome didn't take, the tax collectors claimed was being taken by Rome, and they kept for themselves. The stinking tax collectors grew fatter and fatter like pigs wallowing in their own mire.

He tore his eyes away from the centurion, not wanting to draw any undue attention. He knew that he melted into crowds more easily than most. There was nothing interesting about his bearded face or narrow shoulders. He could be any man . . . a laborer going home for his midday meal, a zealous man going to pray, a family man running an errand. He could be anyone. It was a gift from above, his ordinariness.

Benyamin hunched his shoulders against another gust of wind, driving the dust into his face. Midday. He would report the time.

The image that stayed with him . . . the image that bit into his mind like slivers under his nails . . . was that of the simpering little tax collector grinning. Yes, he had been grinning up at the centurion, smiling up at him like a dog begging for scraps.

May Adonai curse Zacchaeus and all his kin, shrivel their legs and stab out their eyes. May Adonai turn His face from him. And may Adonai remember His true followers . . . the protectors of his Torah . . . the only righteous left in this pagan-stained land.

Oshri was not sure if someone was in the room with him or not.

Voices came to him from a great distance, coming and going as if being blown by a wind.

". . . will not drink . . . tried . . . the fever . . ."

". . . go now . . . it's not late . . ."

"bless us . . . shine down upon . . . hope for your people . . ."

The sound of his mother's voice was louder than the talking. She was singing the same song she'd sung to him and Zacchaeus when they were boys sitting at her skirts, watching her weave. He listened to the voice, sighing in contentment.

"Mother," Oshri said. "I like this song."

He felt a cool hand on his forehead.

And then he was up in that tree, looking down on the world. He looked across the gnarled branches to see his brother grinning back at him. Zacchaeus had the mischievous look on his face of a little kid about to throw a stone. He was dark, browned by the sun on his face and arms. His brother's chest, Oshri knew, was a shade lighter. His hair was brown with dust and there was a smear of dirt on his chin. He wasn't as young as he looked, of course. Zacchaeus had always been small. As a baby he was considered adorable. As a toddler he was disturbingly tiny. As a child, the questions started to fly about why he would not grow. But to Oshri, Zach was his little brother. They were inseparable.

"They're coming!" Zach said, giving a laugh. "Look! I can see them."

Oshri shaded his eyes, but he could not see the road. It was too bright, somehow. He could not make out details. But he could see his brother's laughing excitement.

"I'm going to say something," Zach said.

"Like what?" Oshri asked.

"I'll tell her she's pretty!"

"Bah!" Oshri scratched an insect bite on his leg from his perch in the tree. "You wouldn't dare."

"Watch me!"

Oshri could hear the giggling of approaching girls, but he still could not see anything besides the tree and his little brother looking down, one arm looped around a branch above him and the other drumming on his thigh in nervous expectation.

The scene was growing fuzzy somehow. Oshri saw his little brother slowly fade from view into a dark fog.

"Zach!" Oshri called. "Zach!"

But then it was dark. He could still hear the soft voice singing. He struggled to open his eyes, but the effort seemed too much to manage.

"Hush, son," his mother's voice said gently. "Rest, dear one. You must rest."

"It's dark . . ." Oshri said, or tried to say. He didn't know if his voice had made the words or not.

The soft singing started again, and he struggled once more to open his eyes. He caught a blinding glimpse of his aged mother's face, looking down on him with worried creases around her eyes. But then it was dark again . . . a soft, comforting darkness.

Oh, Elohim, he prayed silently. *Oh, Elohim . . .*

He did not know what he wanted to say. He just wanted to be with Adonai for a moment. But then he almost felt he was spinning, and the comforting darkness swallowed him at last.

λ Living Sign
of Her Sin

Merav looked down her hooked nose at the young man before her. She was tall, thin, and broad shouldered. The lines on her face were deep as plow furrows, and her hands were calloused and large for a woman's. She folded her hands in front of her, her steely gaze directed at the young man. He swallowed hard, his Adam's apple bobbing nervously beneath a patchy beard.

"Aunt, that didn't come out the way I meant it," he protested.

"And how exactly did you mean it, Ravid?" she asked, her voice low and controlled.

"I do not mean that you are old," he began, clearing his throat, and plunging on. "But you are past your . . . your—"

"Prime?" she asked. "Beauty?"

"Fruitful years," he said, shaking his head. "You certainly are still a beauty, Aunt."

"Oh, stop fawning," she muttered. "I am old enough to be your grandmother, and you know it."

Ravid clamped his mouth shut and gave her a thin smile. She'd pressed his patience enough, and she knew it. She was still a woman, albeit a respected woman in her family. She knew her strengths, but she also knew that she relied on this green, young nephew of hers.

"I don't need to be flattered," she said, softening her voice and allowing a smile to come to her lips. "I had my day, boy. I was a beauty before you were ever even thought of. I had a smile that could make a man forget his business."

"Of course, Aunt," he said, running a hand through the bone-straight hair on the top of his head.

Ravid did not believe her, and she nearly laughed out loud. She had never been a beauty, but who would know the difference now? The little lie didn't seem to hurt anything, and it certainly did amuse her. It often happened that gray old things like herself had been pretty in their youth. It just so happened that Merav had actually improved with age. She felt more confident now than she ever had as a young woman with her strong jaw and hooked nose.

"Well then," she said, fixing him with her stare. "Go on. You may leave out the flattery, though."

"Do you want me to say this bluntly?" he asked, annoyance flashing in his eyes.

"Please do," she replied. "I respect the truth over oily flattery."

"You are not a beauty, Aunt," he said, a defiant smile flickering at the corners of his lips. "What you were in your youth I do not know, but I am concerned with who you are now. You are not young, either. You will not be able to give a husband children. Your fruitful days are over. However, you do have a nice little parcel of land that would be appealing to a widower trying to put together an inheritance for some sons. "

"Did you enjoy that?" she asked him, smiling maternally down at him.

"Enjoy what, Aunt?" he asked, his voice chilly.

"Telling the brutal truth to an old woman?"

"Sometimes, Aunt, the truth is what we need to look at," Ravid said, meeting her gaze with angry eyes. "I have a marriage to arrange for you, and you have not made this easy."

"You should be careful how you address me, young man," she said icily. "You may have the duty to provide a marriage for me, but I am still your elder."

"Aunt . . ." he sighed.

"Your mother was dear to me, Ravid," she said quietly. "She bore sons, while I bore only daughters. She was not strong, but I was. I cared for your mother the best I could, young man. You should think twice before insulting me."

Daughters-in-law in the same home . . . married to brothers . . . subservient to a mother-in-law who seemed to be unconvinced that their choice in wives for their sons had been sound. Merav had not been pretty, but she had been strong and stubborn. She knew how to face unhappy times and hold on with her teeth. She learned to hold a stare when she needed to, and how to sidestep a sharp slap. Her prettier, more delicate sister-in-law did not have the same resilience.

"I have not come to insult you, Aunt," Ravid replied, his voice tired. "I came to speak with you about arranging another marriage for you."

"After your uncle, my boy," she said quietly, "it will be hard to move on."

"The family has decided that marriage to a man in our clan would be best," he said, making an obvious effort to keep his voice gentle.

"Because I have no sons to care for me," she finished for him.

"Yes, Aunt."

"And you wish to keep my property within the family," she said.

"Yes, Aunt."

"So who is it that you propose I marry?" she asked.

Ravid was silent.

"You must have a lucky man in mind," she pressed. "I am a woman, and I must obey my family when it decides upon my fate."

"I will have something more solidly planned before I visit you again," he said, bowing his head respectfully. "Until then, may Adonai keep you."

Merav watched as her nephew took his leave. Was it wicked to enjoy toying with this pup the way she did? It likely was, and she cast a half-hearted prayer heavenward, petitioning forgiveness for her fun. But she resented this. She resented being bartered off, a useless old wife but for her piece of land. She resented the oaf she was quite certain they wanted her to wed. She was relatively sure that he was simpleminded. There was only one widower in their clan who was looking to provide an inheritance.

"So that's what I'm worth!" she sniffed. She shook her head and sucked her teeth in suppressed rage.

Merav was no blinking-eyed nanny goat waiting for market. She had desires for her future, and with a little luck and a little conniving she thought she knew how to make it happen.

Ravid clenched his fists as he walked away from his aunt's house. He was her closest kin, and it therefore rested on his shoulders to provide for her. Aunt Merav was a problem. Everyone knew it. She was stubborn, ugly as a bag of stones, and too smart for her own good. She had a brain that had not dulled with age, and that sharp brain was never focused upon woman's work. Yes, Aunt Merav was Ravid's problem.

"Stupid old ewe," he muttered to himself.

Aunt Merav was the woman that King Solomon had warned the future generations of men about. She was the constant drip. She was the nagging crow. She'd been kept in line until the death of her mother-in-law and father-in-law, but upon their deaths she had released her pent up personality like a leashed dog suddenly free. He'd been only a boy when the epidemic came through their village, killing many of the old and young, but he still remembered his Aunt Merav's rise to power in their home.

She had begun with the food. She placed just enough pieces of flatbread for one piece per person. Children who arrived late for dinner did not eat. She had a long, slender stick that she carried about with her and swatted at any child who tried to sneak olives or honey cakes. When Aunt Merav struck, she did so with accuracy and malice.

Ravid remembered the complaints of the men. They said that she talked too much, that she was stingy in her cooking, that she refused to show meekness as was proper. They complained that her bread was hard as wood and that she splashed them when she poured wine from the earthen jug. They muttered that she would not apologize for her indiscretions, but would stare at the man with the sodden sleeve as if it was his fault for getting in the way of the errant wine.

Aunt Merav was a terror.

Ravid's uncle had been no help. He was a gentle man with watery eyes, a stutter, and a pronounced overbite. He would spread his hands and smile a sad smile whenever people complained about his wife.

"I . . . I . . . I . . . I . . ." he'd try to begin. "I . . . d . . . d . . . d . . . don't . . ."

And then he'd stop and spread his hands with that meek smile showing his protruding front teeth. She ruled him like a tyrant, and he didn't seem to mind. That was why his kinsman, Tuvya, seemed like a possible match for the old she donkey. Tuvya's wife had been equally domineering, and the poor old man seemed to mourn her to an obsessive degree. Horrible as it sounded, Ravid was relatively certain that the old man missed his jailor.

If it was a jailor old Tuvya wanted, Ravid had a replacement for him.

Shahar sat silently in the dim room, her face in her hands. She could feel her rough palms against her closed eyes, and her elbows dug into her knees. She could hear the shocked babble of the rest of the family in the house. She knew it was her duty to serve them, but she could not bring herself to rise. The air was thick with old sickness, and the moist hand of death was warm upon the room. Her son lay on that bed. Her firstborn boy.

She lifted her puffy eyes and looked at his peaceful face. She wanted to believe he was sleeping. It would be so much easier if he were simply resting away his illness. But he was not. She hadn't known it was this bad until it was too late. He could not keep any water in his belly. Then when the fever took hold of him, he went into a delirious state. He'd called for her, and she'd recognized the tremor of boyhood. He'd thought he was a little boy still, she was certain, and it made her want to hold him all the more. Her boy . . . her firstborn boy . . .

"What have I done?" she whispered into the room.

What had she done? What had she done to deserve this? To lose a child . . . to lose her eldest son? What sin had she committed to deserve this heartbreak?

She'd known for a long time that she was under Elohim's judgment. She'd known since the birth of her third child, Zacchaeus. The pregnancy had been odd. Her body had not grown to the same extent that it had in previous pregnancies. In fact, she had doubted her condition till quite far along. Zacchaeus had been so tiny at birth that she was afraid that she had miscarried him. He was oddly shapen and half the size of a newborn babe. Yet he survived. At the time she had praised Adonai, believing that her God had given her a gift by allowing her child to live. Instead, He had given her a mark to show her neighbors her hidden sins.

"What happened?" her mother had whispered, looking down at the mewling little thing. "Did you fall?"

Shahar was silent, looking at the tiny infant, his little mouth opening up in hunger, searching. She pulled him to her, shielding his exposed face with her hand. She hated the way her mother was looking at him. She hated to have anyone look at him with anything but love in their eyes. He was tiny. He might not live. But for the days that he survived, she would love him with all her heart.

"She miscarried!"

The word spread around town faster than dust on the wind, settling into the corners, drifting against walls.

"She miscarried, and the poor little thing won't die."

He didn't die. He'd hung on, and eventually he started to grow. She tied him across her body with a length of fabric to keep him close to her while she went about her daily chores, and like any other baby he gurgled and cooed from his cozy little swing.

"I'm sweeping the floor," she'd tell him softly as she worked. "Sweeping to make it clean. That way, when people come into our home, they will know that good people live here, because good people are always clean."

Zacchaeus hadn't grown like other children. He'd stayed small and oddly stunted. He was thick around the chest like the trunk of a tree, and his arms and legs were too short. Yet the boy wouldn't be stopped. Despite his obvious deformity, she'd adored him. He might have been a window into her sinful soul, but he was also her determined little one. He didn't know that he was the mark of her sin.

People would stop and stare at him, their curious, knowing eyes turning from the stunted little boy to his mother. When she stood in the market with him clutching her skirts, she could hear the whispers from the other women.

"Never grew! Her body tried to expel him before the proper time, but the little runt wouldn't die!"

"A living indication of her sins . . ."

"He'll never amount to anything, that's for sure. Never be more than a beggar . . ."

"Because of her. Adonai saw her sins and He brought them out into the light."

Her sins . . . Yes, that was what everyone talked about. What could she possibly have done to deserve this kind of shame? What sin had she committed against God to bring this judgment upon her?

She'd endured. She'd accepted her fate. She'd let them talk. She had accepted her punishment for her grievous sin. Had she not suffered enough? Was Zacchaeus not pain enough for her to bear?

But no, now her firstborn . . . her perfect, beautiful Oshri had been taken from her, too. Would God's hand never lift?

"Why will You not forgive?" she sobbed. "Oh, Adonai, will You ever relent?"

CHAPTER 4

Tzofit's Loss

Chayim rubbed his hands over his face and gave the men around him a tight smile. They sat together in the courtyard of his kinsman, Hevel, their legs curled under them on the brightly woven mats. They were a family. They were kin. Together they faced life and made decisions for their clan. Together they faced this untimely death.

"I have lost a son," he said, tears welling up in his eyes. "But I still have a family."

There was a murmur of assent, and Hevel reached over and clasped Chayim by the ankle, giving him a firm, comforting squeeze.

"Your grief is our grief, brother," Hevel said. "Your son was our son. We have all lost a boy this day."

A servant girl bent beside Chayim, a platter of dates, olives, and cheese held aloft before him in one well muscled arm. Chayim waved her away. She pulled back and gracefully moved to the next man who plucked a handful of food from the plate. Yes, they were kin, and words bound them. Yes, they would grieve together, but no one would feel the pain like Chayim. No other man would be remembering the face of the boy . . . the questions of the young man . . . the excitement of the young groom . . . No other man would be remembering the grown man as the toddler by his mother's skirts.

"Shalom, brothers," Hevel began. "This death has rocked our clan. It is a deep loss."

More nods and murmurs.

"But we are left with a family that must somehow go on with the help of Adonai," Hevel continued. "We are facing challenges. Chayim, would you like to say anything?"

Chayim lifted his eyes to his kinsman and dropped them again. He had nothing to say . . . nothing that would not catch in his throat and pour out with his tears.

"There is the widow to be considered," Hevel said. He let the words hang in the air, and there were some uncomfortable grunts.

"Aye," Chayim sighed. "Tzofit." He scratched his ankle and shifted his position.

"She is—" Hevel began, then stopped.

"A terrible cook," one pointed out.

"Tongue like a viper."

"Stubborn . . . donkey-headed . . ."

"A challenge," Hevel concluded as if he had heard none of the other input.

"Aye," Chayim sighed. "A challenge."

"Not bad looking, though," one man pointed out, glancing apologetically in Chayim's direction. "Would have been hard to tell she'd turn out that way, considering her sweet mother."

"She will need to be provided for," Hevel said.

There was silence.

"Are there any among us looking for wives for their sons?" he asked.

Again, there was silence.

"Lavi?" Hevel said, turning his attention on one thin man with a sparse, gray beard. "Are you not looking for a girl for your second son?"

"I am," Lavi said carefully.

"And would not a nice looking widow like Tzofit be a good match? She is yet to bear children, but she is already knowledgeable in the wifely duties around a home. Your wife would not have to teach her much, I am sure."

"Except for cooking and keeping her mouth shut!" somebody chortled.

"I would be honored to consider such a match," Lavi said, scratching at that sparse beard and pinning his eyes to the mat in front of him. "However, I am already in negotiations for another girl, and would not want to disappoint that family."

"Ah, well," Hevel said, sighing, letting it go. "The truth is, my brothers, that we must provide for our widows. It is the law of Adonai, and the duty of a family. She is young and marriageable. It is inexcusable that she should remain unmarried. We would be scorned by the entire city."

"And what of Zacchaeus?" Lavi said suddenly. "He is unmarried, is he not? The brother of the dead man is duty bound to marry the widow and have children in his brother's name."

"This is true . . ." Hevel said, turning his eyes to Chayim.

Chayim looked back.

"My second son and his sister-in-law despise each other," Chayim said, exhaustion flooding over him. "They are barely civil."

"Marriage is not about gentle words and soft smiles," another man said. "It is about family."

"Are you saying that your son would not obey your order as his father?" Hevel asked.

"I do not say that," Chayim retorted. "I am man of my house, and my word is law!"

"Of course, of course," Hevel said quickly.

"Zacchaeus is a problem all his own," another pointed out. "We have met together before to discuss him."

"His career choice is indeed unfortunate," Hevel replied, diplomatically skirting the issue of his cursed height. "But he is in the position to be able to provide for the widow . . . and to give her children . . ."

All eyes turned back to Chayim. Chayim could see the question there. They were wondering if Zacchaeus could indeed give Tzofit children. In how many ways was Zacchaeus cursed?

"It would be awkward," Chayim said, shaking his head. "With that much hatred between a man and wife, the union could not be a happy one."

"But duty would be done," Lavi insisted.

"Perhaps a good Jewish wife would do Zacchaeus some good," another pointed out. "Besides, with a woman with a tongue like Tzofit's, I highly doubt any union would be happy."

"You chose her, Chayim," someone else said, voice resentful. "It isn't right to try and put her onto one of our homes. You negotiated with her family. You married her to your son. She wasn't our choice."

"I asked your advice!" Chayim retorted. "I asked what you thought, personally."

"Would I try to stop a marriage you obviously wanted so badly?" he demanded. "It was not my place to interfere with your house."

"Bah!" Chayim snapped. "You said she was delightful. You told me that you heard nothing amiss about her. Now you act like I acted alone without any of your input."

"Peace, brothers," Hevel said. "We simply seek for a solution."

"I believe we have one," Lavi murmured.

"Any other suggestions here?" Hevel asked, looking around.

"The brother should marry the widow," another man said, nodding. "It is only proper."

"Agreed," another said.

"Aye, I agree," came another voice.

One by one, the men gave their consent, and Chayim listened in dismay as the voices rang out. There was no pity. Tzofit, it seemed, would be his problem to dispose of.

"And you, Chayim?" Hevel asked, at last.

"What of me?" Chayim asked in misery. "I am an old man who lost his eldest son—"

"Will you consent to the decision of the clan?" Hevel asked. "Will you marry Zacchaeus to Tzofit?"

Chayim held his tongue. His eyes followed the sunlight that dappled the striped mat as it filtered down through the bushy, green leaves of the olive tree. The trunk was thick like intertwined ropes, and the welcome shade extended far into the courtyard. The tree had been rooted in that soil for more than 100 years. Generations had been born, played, grown up, and matured under the shade of this tree . . . and then they had died, and others followed.

"Your home, so filled with grief, will have the laughter of a wedding again, my friend," Hevel said quietly.

Chayim nodded solemnly. Everyone waited.

"I will consent."

There was no choice. The clan had spoken.

"But first," Hevel said sympathetically, "Friend, grieve for your son. There is time enough for weddings, and now there is time enough for grief."

Yes, Chayim would grieve. But now his predominant feeling was one of dread. It was his responsibility to advise Zacchaeus of his upcoming nuptials.

Tzofit was a widow. The thought was a strange one. She'd imagined what widowhood would feel like. She'd pitied widows. They were pathetic. They were needy. Their lot was not enviable. She'd even imagined Oshri dying . . . a sinful, wicked little daydream. But now he was dead. Gone. Resting with his fathers. The illness had taken him, and she found herself unprepared. She found herself in the home of her late husband's family, receiving visitors who came to mourn.

"I'm so sorry," someone was saying in a low voice. "May Elohim be of comfort to you in this time."

She looked up at a familiar face and made some appropriate noises in return.

A widow. No, this was not expected, and she was very aware that she was being observed in the exact way she had observed other widows in times past. They were watching for signs of grief, for excessive shows that might indicate less feeling for her husband than she claimed. For too few tears, or too many. She was being judged on her ability to grieve publicly. However, Tzofit was not grieving.

Guilt wormed in her gut like a wriggling finger. She was shocked, yes. She was worried for her future. She was relieved to be rid of an emotional weight, yet she dreaded this new status—widow. Her own father was dead. She was the property of her in-laws. She was officially a burden.

"Tzofit," a woman said, raising her voice above the mourners wailing outside.

She turned her attention to the woman, a neighbor. She was slender and small with a face like a mouse.

"Hannah, thank you for coming," Tzofit said, her voice tight.

"This must be a terrible time for you," Hannah said. She raised one small hand up to her lips, reminding Tzofit of a mouse cleaning its whiskers.

"Yes, of course," Tzofit said. "It is dreadful. But Adonai must provide."

"Yes, and He will," Hannah said, nodding sympathetically. "He will see how you were to your first husband, and based upon that—"

Hannah paused and cleared her throat. Tzofit's eyes sharpened and she pierced the small woman with a steely glare.

"Yes?" Tzofit said. "You were saying something comforting?"

"I was saying," Hannah said, a gentle smile coming to her lips, "based upon your treatment of your first husband, God will provide a second for you."

"And what do I deserve, Hannah?" Tzofit asked, her tone icy.

"Only you know," Hannah said, shaking her head and pinching her lips together primly. "And Adonai, of course . . ."

Hannah's dark eyes flicked up to meet Tzofit's, and the gentle, breathy demeanor cracked just long enough for Tzofit to see what she dreaded most—gloating. Hannah, Tzofit's dignified and proper neighbor, was glad to see her in this position. Hannah, a woman with a healthy husband and a brood of children that defied her slight build, was enjoying this.

"Tzofit," another woman said, her tone sad, her hands grasping and firm. "May Adonai be your comfort in this time of mourning."

Woman after woman passed by, hands bearing food, lips bearing gossip. Woman after woman passed by, gloating, watching, evaluating, until Tzofit thought she would burst under the scrutiny.

"Tzofit?"

She looked up to see her mother-in-law and for one moment, perhaps the only moment in their lives, Tzofit felt that they were not enemies.

"Come, dear," Shahar said, taking her firmly by the shoulders and urging her to her feet. "You must go rest. The strain will be too much for you."

Tzofit allowed herself to be guided away, listening with a wave of relief to her mother-in-law's expert social maneuvering.

"She is tired, ladies," Shahar said with a sigh. "I am a mother who has lost her son. But Tzofit is a devoted wife who has lost her husband. We both mourn. But Tzofit is much younger than I . . . much more delicate . . ."

"Of course," someone crooned. "You should both rest."

"There is much food," Shahar was saying. "The servants will continue to fill your glasses. Let us retire to pray and weep and we will return to your warm, friendly company."

Tzofit was surprised to feel her mother-in-law's hand remain firmly on her elbow, even out of sight of the guests and into a back room, dim from the covered window that held out the heat. She glanced back in mild alarm at the older woman's creased face, then sucked in her breath in surprise as Shahar spun her around so that they faced each other.

"Mother!" Tzofit gasped.

"You may stop your mocking," Shahar said, her voice tired. "I am weak with grief, but I must keep up appearances."

"We all must, Mother," Tzofit said.

"It would be easier for me if you had loved him," Shahar said, her voice catching with tears. "At least you could show some genuine grief."

"I did!" Tzofit said. "I was dutiful. I did my duty."

Shahar waved her silent.

"I have no strength to cover for your blunders," she said, letting out a shaky sigh. "You are a liability, woman."

"Me?" Tzofit snapped.

"Yes, that temper, right there," Shahar said, jabbing a finger near Tzofit's face. "Right now, my young daughter, we are not only grieving but we are trying to find you a new husband at the same time."

"Yes, Mother."

"You'd better present yourself a little more favorably, my girl," Shahar said, her eyes meeting Tzofit's and holding the stare. "I don't intend to feed you a day longer than I absolutely must!"

With that, Shahar seemed to be drained of all energy. Her shoulders slumped and tears welled up in her eyes. She bit her lip and put one wrist to her forehead. She was crushed, Tzofit could see. She was utterly wounded. She was emptied out by her grief.

Tzofit was not a stone, and the enormity of Shahar's grief was like a punch to the stomach. "Mother," Tzofit said suddenly. "I am sorry . . . I am so sorry."

"For what?" Shahar asked, looking up through her tears, her lips quivering with sorrow.

Tzofit was silent for a moment. Shahar inhaled deeply, her breath shaking, trying to regain control of her emotions.

"For your loss, Mother," Tzofit said, stopping herself from reaching out to the older woman, knowing her touch would not be wanted.

"For my loss?" Shahar asked, shaking her head, giving a wheezing laugh. "But what about your loss, Tzofit? What about yours?"

Tzofit could find no reply.

MERAV

Zaccheus paused before the door of his late brother's home, the sadness welling up in his chest threatening to drown him. As he put his hand on the wooden door worn smooth from blasting wind and grit, he felt as if his brother should be inside, alive and ready to tease. He felt as if he stood here long enough, the past might come back and make his fantasies real.

The door jerked suddenly open and Zacchaeus took an involuntary step backward, glaring angrily up into the face of the servant girl.

"Excuse me, sir," the girl said politely, giving more deference than she normally did. *Probably afraid for her position now that her master is dead*, he thought. "I thought I heard a noise."

He eyed her for a moment, trying to read her practiced, servile expression. Was she expecting someone? Another servant courting her? Or perhaps something as base as a boyfriend?

"My mistress is inside, sir," she said, hesitating slightly.

"Thank you," he said curtly, trying to draw himself up a little taller. Best to get this nasty errand over with. Nothing was ever gained by cringing at a door. He brushed past her and walked inside. This was his father's home, but it was his home, too. He was the only surviving son, and the family house was his by right.

Tzofit stood with her back to him, her spine rigid and her posture erect. When she heard his footsteps, she turned, her lips pressed together and her eyes darting a look of annoyance. She did not look the part of the grieving widow. There were no tears on her cheeks. There was no telltale puffiness under her eyes. Her gaze was not vacant and hollow. *You could at least put on a better show*, he thought bitterly.

"Good evening, sister," he said. "Elohim be with you."

"And with you," she replied, her words short and terse.

"You don't look happy to see me," he said. "I thought you might pretend, at least."

"For what?"

"Your husband is dead, woman," he replied. "Your position is not a solid one."

"Would you believe me if I smiled and fawned?" she asked acidly. "We know each other too well for false pleasantries, brother."

"Perhaps we do," he said with a nod. The thought of Tzofit smiling and fawning turned his stomach. He knew the woman he was dealing with better than most people did. He could hear the sounds of people eating and talking in the courtyard. They were here to support the family in their time of grief . . . and to eat their food, of course. Funerals were an expensive time.

"I should get back to the people," she said, and for a fleeting moment he saw a look of terror in her eyes. She quickly veiled it.

"Then I will say what I have to say quickly," Zacchaeus said. "I wanted to put your grieving heart at ease, sister." His tone was pure sarcasm, and his spite was not lost on her. She met his eyes with a malevolent stare.

"What do you mean?" she asked coldly.

"You will be fed," he said. "You will not be turned out. Some sort of . . . arrangement . . . will be found for you."

"Marriage?" she asked, the hope in her voice unmistakable.

"Or a servant position," Zacchaeus lied, enjoying the look of disbelief and disgust that crossed her face.

"I was your brother's wife!" she hissed.

"Then act the part of a grieving widow, woman!" he retorted. "Or you'll be nothing more than a glorified maid in this house till you die."

"You despise me," she said.

"More than a viper, dear woman. More than a viper."

"Dear brother," she said, her voice turning to honey. "I loathe you even more than the prospect of being a servant."

He nodded his head in exaggerated politeness. "May Elohim keep you."

"And bless you, brother," she replied, dipping her head in return.

Zacchaeus turned and stalked away, heading toward the courtyard where the aroma of food and the sound of chatting voices reached him. She had no fear of him. She'd never bait his father this way. But Oshri never had her respect. No surprise that Oshri's puny brother had even less.

As Zacchaeus kissed his father's cheek in greeting, he wondered how best to make Tzofit as miserable as possible.

The next morning, when the sun had risen high in the sky, Merav adjusted her veil so that it fell in expert folds over her shoulders. She'd learned as a young woman how to adjust her clothing to diminish her too prominent physical attributes . . . like her shoulders, her towering height, and her broad hands. A face was easily hidden behind a veil, but other things required more cunning.

She sighed. There was no hiding what she was. If age had taught her anything, it was that a body and a face did not change except to stoop, wrinkle, and toughen. Your body and that face simply accompanied you through your lifetime. Might as well accept them, care for them, and get comfortable with them because ridding yourself of either was impossible.

She sat in Zacchaeus' courtyard, sipping quietly on a cup of wine. It was excellent, not that she expected anything less. Zacchaeus was known for his good taste, if nothing else. But what he was known for didn't bother her. She had always seen something . . . attractive . . . in this man.

"Madam," a voice said, and she quickly looked up to see Zacchaeus walking toward her. He had a sad, but easy smile. His beard was well cropped and he moved with a grace that showed he, too, was comfortable in the body he had been dealt. She quickly appraised his robe, noticing the expensive cut and drapery.

"Good morning, sir," she said, looking down politely. "I hope I did not bother you too early."

"No, no," he said, waving his hand. "Of course not. I'm sorry that I didn't come immediately to greet you, but I was occupied with my brother's estate."

"My condolences," she said.

"Thank you." He stopped, frowned, gestured to a servant, then arranged himself opposite her on a mat. He leaned forward, his dark eyes meeting hers frankly.

"I thought there would be other guests, or I would have brought a chaperone," she excused herself.

"They are at my father's home. I am not a favorite for visitors, I can assure you."

"Yes, I know," she said matter-of-factly, inwardly cringing when she saw his look of surprise.

"You don't chop words," he said, an amused smile curling the corners of his lips.

"Sir," she said. "I can be as gracious as I must, but there are times that glossing over a bare fact seems like a waste of time."

"And the fact remains that I am next to shunned in many circles," he replied, the smile remaining on his lips.

"Your occupation would do that," she said with a nod.

"Is there anything else about me that would cause such a reaction?" he asked, baiting her with wide, mock-innocent eyes.

She rolled her eyes at him, and he burst into laughter.

"Madam," he said, shaking his head, "you have made me laugh today, and for that I will remain grateful." He glanced at a servant approaching with a platter of dried fruit and cheese curds. "Please, have something to refresh you."

"I think I understand you," she said after taking some food in her hand.

"How so?" he asked. "It seems a little impertinent for a woman to claim she understands the mind of a man."

"I wouldn't dream of rising above my position as a woman," she demurred. "I do not understand your business or the world of men, of course."

That was a lie. She understood his business perfectly, and the world of men was not so convoluted and mystifying as many women seemed to believe. But this was not the time to tell a man that he did not awe her with his very presence. She had brain enough for that.

"Go on," he encouraged.

"Let me tell you what I see." She pursed her lips in thought. "I see a lonely man. You have an exquisite home and the exquisite taste of a king, but no guests to appreciate it. Your whole life you have been told that you are not attractive. I understand that because I, too, have been criticized for my looks. I will not pretend otherwise. For your short stature, I am a virtual giant. I know how words sting."

Zacchaeus let out a sound somewhere between a grunt and a chuckle. She met his eyes with an honest smile.

"A friend is a good thing to have, sir," she said finally.

He nodded silently, looking down into his cup and chewing the side of his cheek.

"Am I so transparent?" he asked.

"No, only to one who has felt the same things," she said.

"But you were married, were you not?" he asked.

"I was," she said. "And I made him happy, I am proud to say. But he is gone now, may Adonai bless him, and the kin who are responsible for me resent me."

"Why?" he asked.

"Oh, for many things," she admitted quietly. "For being intelligent. For knowing how to manage a home that had too little money, a home that wanted to pretend to have more than it did."

"Ah!" he said with a laugh. "No one wants to be reminded of their station."

"And for giving birth to girls," she said.

"Unforgivable," he chided.

"I know," she said, catching the laughter in his voice and chuckling. "But they are sturdy girls who know how to cook and make the most of their husbands' homes. Not the prettiest, but certainly smarter than the clucking hens."

"I'd believe it," he said. "Are they all married?"

"Curious for yourself?" she asked, trying to hide the catch in her breath.

"Marriage . . ." he waved his hand. "I can't say that I don't sometimes wish for a woman to make this place a home, but . . ."

"But?" she urged.

He shook his head, remaining silent.

"They are all married," she affirmed after a moment. "All eight."

"Eight girls!" He let out a low whistle. "No wonder they resent you."

She sniffed and laughed softly.

"I'm not beautiful," she added quietly.

He waved his hand dismissively. "Of course, you are."

"Kind of you to be polite," she said. "But since we are being honest—"

"Then, in the spirit of honesty, I should inform you that I am short," he said, catching her eye with a wink. "Short and cursed, if you listen to the old wives' talk." She couldn't help but laugh at this and they chuckled together.

"Madam," he said.

"Please, call me Merav," she said. "It is my name, and I consider you a friend."

"Then call me Zacchaeus," he said, giving her a warm smile. "Merav, you don't know what your visit has done for me today."

"Perhaps we could visit again," she said. "We are both in need of . . . friendship."

"It would seem we are," he said with a slow nod. "It would seem we are."

If she were younger, Zacchaeus would have been uncomfortable with their banter. He would have felt the need to put her in her place. He would have flirted, then said something cruel before she could give him a look of disgust or rejection. But this was not a young woman. This was not a pretty woman. Even she knew the reality of her state. He couldn't help but like her.

"Did you know Oshri, my brother?" he asked.

"Not well, I'm sorry to say."

"You should have," he said, smiling sadly to himself. "He was . . . how to describe him . . ."

"I had six brothers," she supplied quietly.

"Then perhaps you understand," he said. "A brother is close."

"Very," she agreed. "I think it was obvious how close you and Oshri were. Even those of us who were not intimate with your family could see your bond."

He nodded and sighed.

"You looked alike," she said.

"Oshri and I?" he asked, looking up in surprise.

"In the eyes," she confirmed. "And the shoulders."

"I always thought we looked like relative strangers," he said with a shake of his head.

"Oh no," she said. "You were brothers. There was no denying it!"

"That's a comfort," he said quietly. "Odd the things that comfort you at a time like this . . ."

He looked up at the woman in front of him. Her face was lined, but her eyes were intelligent and compassionate. Her shoulders were wide for a woman's and she was thin as a rope, but she folded her hands rather elegantly in her lap. She was old enough to be his mother, he guessed, if she'd started having children quite young. He couldn't quite identify what he felt toward her, how he related to her. But "friend" was likely the best description he felt.

"Would you like to come for a dinner at my home some evening?" he asked suddenly, the words coming out in a rush. "I understand, of course, if you have other obligations . . . people are so busy these days."

He stopped speaking and looked at her, suddenly quite terrified of her response.

"I would be very pleased to come, Zacchaeus," she said with a smile that lit up her face. "Very pleased, indeed."

"Then I will send an invitation," he said, returning her smile.

Zacchaeus felt, for the first time in a long time, happy.

CHAPTER 6

THE DECISION

Chayim watched as his wife, Shahar, poured some wine for a guest, her arms shaking under the strain of supporting the heavy pitcher. She had lost weight since the death of their son, and strength, too. Only a week ago she would have easily hoisted that pitcher in one hand without a change in her breathing. She hadn't been eating, Chayim suspected. Her grief was overwhelming her and she was not caring for herself the way she should. She looked up, noticed him watching her, and gave her husband a small smile.

Shahar's name meant "dawn." It was a good name for her. She was a beautiful woman—still beautiful after all these years. She had been an excellent choice by Chayim's father. Dutiful, obedient, silent when the occasion called for it. Even during the mourning of her eldest son, Shahar was acting like a proper woman. She was serving. She was anticipating the needs of her guests. She was saving her own grief for privacy later, when even her husband would not witness it. From looking at her . . . from watching her propriety . . . you would never guess that she harbored some terrible sin. It was a sin that even Chayim did not know about, but that became evident at the birth of their misshapen son.

The house was full . . . guests still arriving, come to give their support to the grieving family. The smell of garlic and coriander from the simmering lentils wafted toward Chayim from the courtyard. Baked gourds, cucumbers with vinegar, broad beans, and goat seasoned with mustard and mint were among the dishes being served. The savory smells turned his stomach and he swallowed hard.

"You wanted to speak with me, Father?" Zacchaeus asked, and Chayim jerked, startled, then looked at his younger son. His only son.

"I do," Chayim said, putting a hand on his son's shoulder. "Come outside where we may have some privacy."

The two men angled in the direction of the door, nodding to

some guests just entering the house. They paused, exchanged some pleasantries, accepted condolences, and shuffled out into the night air. Chayim sighed, looking out into the darkness.

Elohim . . . if only there were another way, he prayed silently. But there was not another way and Chayim was not a foolish man.

The moon was a faint sliver, but the stars were bright and the breeze refreshingly cool. He breathed deeply through his nose and pressed his lips together.

"Father?"

Chayim looked down at Zacchaeus' face. Gray already speckled the hair at his temples. He saw the immaculately groomed beard. He saw the worried eyes. The body had grown, the hair had sprouted and begun to change color, the voice had deepened, but the eyes remained the same since boyhood . . . the same questioning eyes that did not understand.

"I have made a decision," Chayim said brusquely.

There was silence as a response.

"You will be married soon," Chayim said.

Emotions passed over his son's face. Dismay melted into curiosity, changed to a tentative happiness, and then settled back into worry.

"Do you have any questions?" Chayim asked. "Or are we done here?"

"Father," Zacchaeus said, putting a hand on Chayim's arm. "Is this a . . . good idea?"

"Do you question me?" Chayim asked, irritated.

"Never, Father," Zacchaeus said, frowning and pressing his lips together.

"We must deal with this as a family, son," Chayim said, softening. "I know you won't like this, but it's proper. She must be provided for."

Zacchaeus' eyes widened. He froze for a moment, then violently shook his head.

"No!" he cried, his eyes flashing fire. "You aren't saying—"

"Tzofit must be provided for," Chayim said. "She is your brother's widow, and she must bear children in your brother's name."

"Father, I do not blame you for choosing her for Oshri," Zacchaeus said carefully. "But knowing what we know of her now . . ."

"She is still ours, son!" Chayim snapped. "That will not go away!"

The clan was not going to forget, and Tzofit was not going to evaporate with the morning dew. The problem remained. Tzofit had been his choice . . . his only choice in a daughter-in-law. She had been his mistake, and Oshri had paid for it. She was their burden to bear.

"She's sharp tongued, angry, insolent, a terrible cook—"

"Shut your mouth, Zacchaeus," Chayim said, struggling to keep his tone under control. "Do not slander her name. She is your brother's widow and will soon be your wife."

"Father!" Zacchaeus opened and shut his mouth twice, as if unable to push the words out.

Chayim was not a hard man. He felt his son's misery. Tzofit was not a woman he would have liked to take to wife, either, and he didn't like being the father forcing his son into a dreaded match. He preferred to be the father arranging a marriage that made his son thankful. But Zacchaeus would never have been an easy son to arrange a marriage for. No, any other woman who could be acquired for him would be incredibly low in social standing. She would be an embarrassment in other ways. Better the dog they knew than the wild mutt off the street.

"It will not be all misery, son," Chayim said, his tone softening. "A woman need not be a burden. Amuse yourself outside of the house. Never give her a moment's softness. Let her know that you are her master. Your brother was too soft on her. A strong hand will tame that one."

Zacchaeus looked doubtful, but all that this son knew about marriage could fit in a thimble. Marriage brought wisdom of its own.

"I know I have shamed you, Father," Zacchaeus said, his voice tight.

Chayim waved his hand, and his son dropped back into silence.

"You owe me obedience," Chayim said.

Zacchaeus looked in his eyes, his face set like stone.

Did his son hate him? What words was he biting back behind that clenched jaw? Did he not know that Chayim had no choice, either?

"It won't be all misery, son," Chayim repeated, and he loathed the sound of pleading in his own voice.

That same night, across the twisting streets of Yericho, another group of men sat together late into the night. Clouds of smoke from the oil lamps drifted throughout the room. The lamps sputtered from time to time as the flame hit impurities, fingers of black smoke rising from the wicks and little clay bowls. *The impure oil is like Judah,* Benyamin thought . . . *once pure and unspoiled, she now was laced with filth.* It was cheap oil there in the lamps. Common. Filthy. He could smell it, but he was not one to complain about physical discomfort. The body mattered little. What mattered was the spiritual.

The small room was ripe with the odor of sweating bodies, stale breath, and sputtering lamps. A leather flap at one window had been thrown back to let in a breeze, but so far the breeze seemed to by-pass the small opening. The men sat around a low table with a meager fare before them. There was day old flatbread, some dried dates, olives that looked bruised, and a bowl of beans. The men were not a wealthy group, at least not by appearance. They ranged in age from an elderly man, skin as thin as garlic paper, to a young man barely out of his youth, his cheeks still downy with his first beard. Benyamin tore a piece of flatbread for himself and bit into the tough crust.

"The Messiah *will* come!" one man was saying. "He will come and obliterate the Romans . . . Their men will be murdered, their women will be taken into slavery, and their children will be exiled to walk the desert alone with no adult to care for them until they fall to the searing sand with hunger."

Benyamin felt a smile coming to his lips at this familiar prediction.

"Yes, but we must be ready for his appearance," Benyamin pointed out. "We must be found worthy."

"Israel has become weak," another spat. "Weak and pathetic. All they care about is the accumulation of coins and the betrothals of their children."

"They have turned from Adonai," the young man said, his voice cracking. He blushed and angrily grit his teeth.

"Adonai punished Israel for her filth and degradation," the old man said, his voice quivering with the effort of being heard. "Allowed her enemies to wipe her up like spilled wine . . ."

"Yericho deserves to be burned to the ground like Sodom,"

Benyamin said, his voice low. "This city deserves to be torched and left empty."

There was an uncomfortable silence.

"We cannot punish people without proof of their guilt," someone said. "We are but men, and mistakes can be made."

"Mistakes in good faith," Benyamin retorted.

"Son," the old man said, "I admire your zeal for the Lord, but it must be tempered. It must be directed toward the vile Gentiles, not toward your fellow Judeans."

"What if the Judean has sold out his brothers?" Benyamin asked, looking around the table at the curious faces. "What about the tax collectors?"

A general grumbling of disgust rumbled around the table.

"Sell us out is what they do!" someone said. "Cower before the heathen swine and turn on their own kind. They are a waste of Elohim's breath."

"I have been watching one in particular," Benyamin said, his gaze flicking from man to man. "He's hideous! Not only is he a tax collector, wealthy from theft, but he is also a mutant."

"A mutant?" someone asked, frowning.

"Freakishly small. You've never seen a man like this," Benyamin insisted, casting his gaze excitedly around the room. "What his mother did to cause her husband's seed to be so deformed we can only imagine. The man has been steeped in sin since his mother's womb! He is no larger than a child, but has the hair and voice of a grown man."

"A sign from Adonai," someone agreed. "What was done in secret will certainly be made known."

"And this little freak robs good Jews of their bread so that he can live in lavish luxury," Benyamin spat. "It turns my stomach to even see it!"

"Something should be done," the youngest said, his eyes glittering in the smoky light.

"Something that tells him Adonai does not condone his flagrant sin!" another retorted.

There was another uncomfortable silence.

Benyamin lowered his eyes. "I want to kill him," he said quietly.

He lifted his head and looked at the plastered wall, his eyes following a long crack that disappeared into a corner. He finally drew his gaze back to the men at the table. They looked back at him, their faces mirroring a mixed response. The youngest's eyes had lit up in pleasure. The oldest looked undecided. Two men looked fearful while the others appeared cautiously approving.

"Rabbi?" one of the men said, turning to the oldest. He sat with his eyes shut, his knobby, bent fingers fiddling with his white beard.

"Adonai's Torah must be kept," the old man said finally. "Those who do not must be eradicated. Elohim ordered that all of the heathen be destroyed in the Promised Land. It is a command."

"This is different than fighting soldiers, Benyamin," an older man said softly.

"Tax collectors are swine!" Benyamin barked back. "Filthy pigs. If you'd seen him. If you'd seen the way he was grinning up at the Romans . . ."

He had to stop. He felt the old rage flooding into him again, filling him up and swallowing him whole. Why could they not see it? Why would they not cheer their enthusiasm that one more tax collector was going to be dead? A dead tax collector was as good as a dead Roman.

"He is a sinner," the rabbi said. "He must be treated as such. His parents must be grievous sinners, too, to have sired such a child."

Benyamin stopped paying attention to the discussion. They were working themselves up to it. Their devotion to the Torah was weak. Benyamin was different, though. He had known since he was a child that he must defend the Torah. He knew that Elohim's holy words must be uplifted. He knew that sinners had no place with Adonai's people, and that only when they were willing to take the ultimate stand would He look down on them with favor. Those who simply sacrificed and closed their eyes to the evil bathing their nation were sadly mistaken if they thought that Adonai would be pleased with them. It took more than a sacrifice to please the Creator.

He knew. He knew the pain, the denial, the work it took to please the Almighty. If anyone knew, it was Benyamin.

"Who will do this?" the rabbi finally asked.

All eyes turned to Benyamin. He closed his eyes and took a slow, deep breath, willing calmness back into his mind.

"I will," he said quietly. "I volunteer myself."

Oh God of Abraham, Isaac and Jacob, he prayed in his heart. *Bless the work of my hands. Provide me the opportunity I require. Give this sinful animal into my hands. To You be all glory!*

CHAPTER 7

Two Hurting Women

Gaius Markus Africanus stopped midstride and turned away from the little tax collector's door, his attention arrested by the form of a slim young woman slipping past him. She carried a bundle of baked goods on her head, balanced by one hand. Her eyes were fixed on the path ahead of her with a grim sort of determination, and she bit her bottom lip as if deep in thought. Her cheeks were flushed from the heat of the sun, and she was breathing quickly, obviously in a hurry. Hers were beautiful eyes, eyes with long dark lashes and deep, deep centers that begged him to dive into them, drown in them. She was stunning, truly lovely. He was a man who had seen a great many women, enjoyed a great many women. This woman was easily the most beautiful of them all.

Today Gaius came to the home of Zacchaeus about business alone. He was not transporting taxes, did not require any foot soldiers as accompaniment, and he took the luxury of watching a beautiful girl for a few moments longer.

He fiddled with the leather sheath of his short sword, running his calloused fingers over the smooth, oiled leather as he smiled to himself. He stood with his legs akimbo, feeling the heat of the day baking against his back, burning the backs of his legs. She surely was a pretty thing. The Jews certainly had some gorgeous women, and this particular woman was something to behold. Those eyes . . . the plump lips . . . the delicate feet . . . a slender wrist and forearm . . .

Gaius was a centurion. This alone was enough to give him the courage to approach any woman he desired, given that her position wasn't too elevated, but Judeans were a different story. Being a centurion wouldn't recommend him to this girl. And even if he were . . . what? Even if he were whatever Judean women might secretly desire . . . a rabbi? A merchant? Even if he were of her Jewish faith, these women weren't known for their . . . availability.

Stupidly, it made her all the more desirable.

The young woman paused in her trek, tugging at her veil that had slipped back on her head revealing a soft, black curl that tumbled down her cheek. She tucked it quickly away, took the bundle off her head and rearranged the coarse fabric over her hair, expertly folding and tucking it around her face and neck. Her gaze moved uncertainly around as she readjusted herself, and as she was bending to pick her bundle up again, her eyes, those dark, searching eyes, fell on Gaius.

"Good morning, miss," he said, allowing a smile to warm his face.

She looked at him stricken, frozen in her position as if she hoped she would blend in with the cobbles of the street.

"It's a hot day," he said. "Don't you think?"

She was still silent, but now her hands were moving, feeling in front of her for the loaves that now tumbled out of the cloth that had secured them. Her lips moved wordlessly, and as soon as she picked up a loaf it would fall out of her faltering fingers and bounce back to the ground. Gaius saw a street urchin moving in to grab what he could.

"Hey!" he barked. The coarse sound of his voice frightened the boy off, but it seemed to have the same effect on the young woman who appeared about to abandon her ware and disappear.

"I'm sorry," he said, adjusting his tone. "The street rat . . . the boy . . . I didn't want him to steal your bread."

Her hands seemed to cooperate now, and she plucked the small loaves up off the ground and back into the cloth, wrapping it tightly around the bread once more, pushing herself to her feet.

"Wait!" Gaius called, but she had already turned and was dashing away down the street, casting frightened looks behind her until she dodged around a corner. Gaius did not give chase, but he watched her. No, he was a not a ruffian to chase a woman down in the street. He was civilized. He was Roman. And he'd just seen the woman of his dreams.

He sighed and smiled ruefully to himself. Those were lips he would have liked to kiss. That was a curl of hair he would have liked to twine around his finger. Nothing made a man feel more like a man than pursuing a beautiful woman.

Unwelcomed, the image of his wife rose up in his mind and he sucked his teeth and shook his head. Clodia was a beautiful woman, too . . . but she did not have the youth. She had born him seven children. Her body and figure had softened with motherhood, her hair had grayed at the temples, and her flawless skin had started to line and crease, betraying lines of bitterness instead of laughter.

He hated himself for the feeling of dread that dropped into his stomach. It was her bitterness than unnerved him. Her quiet questioning with eyes filled with loathing. Her looks, oozing resentment, when he mentioned another woman. As if she had a right to question what he did to amuse himself!

Stories were told of virtuous Roman wives . . . stories that were told mother to daughter for generations, meant to give the example of femininity that their mothers could not give by example alone. Two stories came to his mind, and he remembered the sound of his mother's voice as she had told them to his sisters. He allowed himself a smile for the boy who used to sit around corners, listening to the strange education of girls.

There was once a wife of such virtue that when her husband's attention was drawn to one of her serving girls, she did not get jealous or angry. In fact, she knew that her husband was so much her superior that she could not imagine criticizing him, even in her mind. She served her husband faithfully through life, and when he was taken from her in a tragic accident, she mourned him deeply. Even after his death, she felt no jealousy or anger toward the serving girl who had monopolized so much of her husband's attention during his life. In fact, she allotted the girl a certain amount of money to keep her comfortably through life and requested that she be set free. Such was her feminine virtue.

There was another story of a Roman citizen convicted of treason. He was sentenced to death, but since he was a citizen and not a barbarian, he was commanded to end his own life in a certain number of days. The thought of death terrified him. The days passed, and he could not make his move. He could not take his own life. The day before the deed would be done for him if he failed to comply his devoted wife took a dagger from her robes and put it against her chest, planning to give her husband the courage to do what he must with the dignity of a Roman.

"It will not be so bad, my husband," she said. "You will see." And she plunged the dagger into her chest.

As she slumped to the ground, the dagger falling from her fingers, she said, "See? It doesn't hurt at all."

That was a wife. *That* was a woman.

Why, in the name of Jupiter, did Clodia refuse to be a proper Roman matron?

Clodia looked at her reflection in the oval mirror propped up on top of her vanity table. Various trinkets lay strewn over the top of the table . . . a bracelet with a broken clasp, several bottles and tubs of ointments and paints, a cloth covered in smudges. She held a comb in one hand, but she sat motionlessly, gazing at the face in the mirror.

"I have aged," she said softly. Years before, when she was still young and vain, she had been able to stare into a mirror and see nothing but beauty. Now a woman in her forties, she looked into the mirror and saw the same features, some extra lines, some sagging, but she was not able to put the details together into anything so subjective as beauty or ugliness. She saw herself. She saw the years that had passed. She saw a woman she had made her peace with.

Her hair was carefully coiled, pinned, oiled, and arranged on the top of her head, a few gold strings entwined through the curls. A bejeweled broach held her robe together at one shoulder. She looked down at her hands, then opened a jar and dabbed her fingers into the cool salve. She smoothed it over her hands using long, measured strokes, one hand and then the other . . . one hand and then the other.

She heard some movement behind her and glanced up to see a slave girl holding a tray with some watered wine in a goblet. Clodia did not see the slave, however. She saw only the wine. She looked back down to her hands and continued to massage them, willing the aging to reverse. The wine was set next to her, and soon she was alone again.

Ten pregnancies took its toll on a body. Her middle was expanded and soft. She drooped. She sagged. Her body had delivered life and sucked the last of her youth out of her. Seven babies had survived out of the 10. One died at birth. It was a boy, but he was too weak to face the world and instead turned back to cross the River. The second to die was a girl. She lived for two years, but then caught a fever and was gone in one night, crossing the River in the midst of tangled sheets and murmuring doctors. The third . . . the third was the baby that haunted her.

"A boy?" Gaius had asked, his dark eyes locked on hers.

Clodia had let her head drop back to the bed. Her heart was racing and she could feel the tears welling up inside of her. Her body ached and burned from the delivery, and her arms longed to hold the little one. But the baby was in the nurse's arms, sleeping peacefully. It was not Clodia's job to nurse the baby. It was her job to recover so that she could continue in her wifely duties.

"Well?" Gaius had repeated. "A boy?"

Clodia hadn't answered him. She just looked up mutely, her lips quivering. She tried to push herself up in the bed, but the pain stopped her, twisting in her gut. This birth had been a bad one. It had done something awful to her, she knew.

Gaius had stood before her bed for what seemed like an eternity. His face was an iron mask, but his fists kept flexing. She knew he was battling himself. He was facing something within in the same way he faced a barbarian horde. He was reaching down within himself for the brutality necessary to win.

"Husband," she said, her voice shaking. "She is so pretty. If you would just look at her . . ."

"Silence!"

She obeyed. She had no choice. She looked toward the nurse who stood immobile, lips pressed together in a thin line and eyes staring vacantly ahead. Clodia reached her arms toward the baby, but the nurse did not see. Clodia let her arms drop as the tears trickled down her cheeks.

"Oh, Gaius!" she pleaded. "Please! Don't do this to me!"

His eyes turned toward her, and for a moment she thought he might relent. His face softened and his eyes once more held the tenderness of years ago. But as quickly as it came, the look fluttered away like a moth, leaving his face vacant and impassive.

"Expose it," he said, his voice sounding hoarse and forced.

Clodia watched as her husband turned and stalked woodenly from the room. And she was left with the little girl . . . the tiny mewling infant that would not be permitted to live.

Now, a year later, her throat still closed with grief and longing at the thought. She had been so tiny, with a shock of black hair and a little nose that turned up. Her tiny mouth kept searching for milk. At the time, being so near after a birth, Clodia did not remember loving the baby yet. She remembered feeling panic-stricken and anxious. She remembered feeling emotional. But the feeling of deep, maternal love came later. It came with day after day of remembering that tiny girl with her black hair standing straight up and the tiny mouth searching . . . searching . . . the thin, newborn cry.

Clodia stopped massaging her hands and looked into the mirror. The eyes burned with hatred and the lips were turned down in loathing. He could not abide any more girls, he had said. He would only accept boys from this point onward.

Clodia pushed herself to her feet and took a deep breath. She crossed the room to a small shrine. A statue of a woman wearing chainmail stood in the midst of some wilting flowers. The hair on the statue's head was depicted in feminine curls, and in one hand the statue held a spear. With its head under one of her hands, a deer looked adoringly up at her. Clodia knelt before the shrine and closed her eyes. She breathed deeply, her shoulders relaxing and her hands going limp in her lap.

"Oh, Minerva," she intoned. "Goddess of wisdom, medicine, and crafts . . . Oh, Minerva, mother, huntress, virgin . . ."

Clodia's voice trailed away, and she was left breathing . . . breathing . . .

"Oh, Minerva, goddess of poetry, inventor of music . . . sprung whole from the mind of Jupiter . . ."

Clodia could hear the far away sounds of the household. She could hear the steady clunking of wagon wheels, the hum of orders being given, orders being followed. She felt the breeze coming across the room to her from a high window. She could hear the whine of a gnat somewhere near her head.

"Of all the goddesses, you would hear me," Clodia said quietly. "Of all the goddesses, you would avenge me . . ."

She bowed, pressing her forehead against the cool tile floor. Her knees ached in the posture, but she remained in that position for several moments more before pushing herself back into a seated position.

"Oh, Minerva," she sighed. But she did not know what to ask. She did not know what would take away her pain. She did not know who she hated more . . . her husband, the women who bewitched him, or herself. She did not have the words to describe her feelings. She did not have the words to encompass her misery. The only words she had kept spilling from her lips.

"Oh, Minerva, goddess of wisdom, medicine, and crafts . . . Oh, Minerva . . . Mother, huntress, virgin . . ."

Tzofit put a woven lid over a tray of flatbread to keep the flies away and stood up, wiping the sweat from her forehead with the corner of her veil. The oven was outside in the courtyard, but that did not keep its heat from hitting her like a wall and making her drip with perspiration. She felt a trickle down her back, but it did nothing to relieve her misery. On the other side of the courtyard, under the shade of the ancient olive tree, with its trunk like twisted ropes and its boughs like gnarled fingers, she half heard the voices of the men deep in discussion.

Zacchaeus sat across from his father. Several cousins were present as well. They sat cross-legged, their legs exposed and their hands gesturing in a passionate argument. One of the men stood up, paced back and forth, then turned his back on the others. Another went to mollify the man who had left the group, and those two began a heated discussion filled with hand gestures and exclamations. After a few minutes they returned to the group and the arguing continued.

This was a normal family gathering. Men were passionate creatures, their feelings worn on the sleeves of their robes. If an emotion entered into any of their heads, it would be declared openly before they even thought. That was the world of men. Tzofit was a woman, and she covered her emotions with layer upon layer of practice, subtlety, and veiling. A good and proper woman could be stripped of her veil and still hide her emotions. Her feelings were not to be a burden to others. Men might display every passing feeling with no shame, but Tzofit knew better.

She hoisted the platter of flatbread, pausing for a moment to get the balance before walking toward the group of men, her eyes cast demurely down. The men wanted to at least appear like they were speaking privately, even though their voices carried. She lowered the platter, feeling her muscles quiver under its weight.

". . . family is family," one cousin was declaring. "Kin is kin."

"And a poor business decision still loses money, regardless of who makes it!" Zacchaeus snapped.

"I don't think that you are part of this decision, young man," an older man said, his voice dripping disdain.

"He is my heir," Chayim sighed.

"And our local tax collector," someone added.

"He will not inform on us," Chayim said. "We are kin."

"And who came to collect from me after I privately purchased a small plot of land?"

"Privately?" Zacchaeus laughed. "I thought you were begging to be taxed the way you were bragging about it to every stranger who passed by. Had I not taxed you, I would have been showing obvious favoritism."

"The point is," another cousin said, "he has conflicting interests."

Zacchaeus looked up at Tzofit, and for a moment, just one fleeting moment, she felt what it would be like to be the wife of this little man. She felt the rage at seeing him disrespected. She saw the embarrassment of being labeled his wife. She saw how shaky their joint interests would be. And as he lifted his eyes and locked them onto hers, she expected to see a similar realization dawning in his glance, too.

Tzofit was wrong, however. All she saw in Zacchaeus' eyes was annoyance and disgust.

"Why are you here, sister?" he snapped. "A woman's place is not eavesdropping on men's discussions. Get back to the fire!"

His words jolted her back into the present, and she felt her cheeks grow hot with rage and humiliation. She spun on her heel and retreated, doing her best not to scurry.

The family expected her to marry Zacchaeus. She knew it! To find another bride willing to take the stunted tax collector would be impossible unless the girl crawled off the streets. So Tzofit was the only other option. She was widowed. She had no choice. Her in-laws, who despised her as much as she despised them, would match her to her brother-in-law, and she would be forced to be wife to a man she loathed.

In the marketplace, people sold doves and other small birds in baskets. When you passed by their booths you could hear the pathetic fluttering, the scrape of feathers against dry rushes. You could hear the confused cries of the fowl. It had always made her pity the poor creatures that were doomed to be sacrificed or made into soups.

But now she felt like a dove in a basket. She had no choice. She had no way of escape. Those who jostled her and slammed down the lid did not care for her comfort. They didn't care for her preferences or her feelings. All they cared was that propriety was maintained, that they did not appear to be shirking their duties. And when that lid descended over her head, Tzofit felt all of her emotions rise to a boiling point. She wanted to scream. She wanted to claw at the lid. She wanted to bite and fight and run away.

And something inside of her wanted to pray . . . but words would not encompass what she felt. They could not express the confusion of her emotions. They could not articulate her anxiety, her fear, her hatred. And so she prayed the only words that were left inside of her . . .

"Blessed are You, Lord our God, King of the Universe, who creates fruit of the ground."

It was a blessing on vegetables.

CHAPTER 8

There Would Be Hope

In one hand Bracha held the cloth that had covered her rounds of freshly baked bread. She allowed her eyes to scan the crowds of people in the Yericho streets. She didn't see the centurion, and she was glad. But she had seen him several times the last couple of weeks, and each time his attention was locked on her. She shivered. Today he had tried to speak to her.

Romans! She did not understand them, nor did she care to. They were the occupiers. They were the pagans. They were the pig-eating, crucifying, torturing barbarians that the Messiah would rid them of! Her brother talked about it often enough to make her feel like she'd read the prophesies about the Messiah herself. Of course, she could not read, but her brother, Benyamin, had learned to cipher and he had read actual scrolls on several different occasions. He was the most learned person she knew, besides the rabbis, of course.

Bracha followed the narrow, twisting street, hopping over the familiar potholes and piles of animal excrement, dodging other pedestrians and carts. The smell of cooking fires, dung, dust, sweat, and burned beans hung over the district in a haze. She pulled her veil closer over her face, but this was out of modesty, not disgust of the odor of the streets. She'd lived in this district of Yericho all her life so the stench of poverty meant nothing to her.

"Bracha!" some small children called, and she stopped to ruffle their hair. They grinned up at her with dirty faces. "Anything left over?" they asked.

"Not today," she told them, feeling a pang of guilt for not saving a few crusts for the little ones. "I'm sorry. I'm sure there'll be something tomorrow."

They scattered immediately, their disappointment not lasting long. They'd scavenge somewhere else. These were children who were accustomed to disappointment, and they knew that sulking only wasted precious begging time, and their distended little bellies were empty.

Bracha stopped at a little hut with an open door. In the front of the tiny building was a cooking fire and an old woman was stirring a barley stew with a long handled spoon with a broken end. She looked up at Bracha and gave her a toothless smile.

"Mama," Bracha said, stopping to kiss her mother's leathery cheek. "Let me help you."

"How much did you get?" her father asked sharply.

Bracha reached under her robe to a small pouch of pennies which she untied and wordlessly passed to her father. He pried the drawstring open and turned his back to peer into the depths, shielding the few pennies from the view of any prying observer.

"This is it?" he demanded. "What did you buy, you little tramp?"

"I didn't buy anything, Abba!" she said, tears welling up in her eyes. "This was all I could get. It's all I ever get!"

"You would argue with me?" he retorted, pushing himself to his feet, but favoring one sore leg. He raised a hand as if to strike her, but she stepped away, ducking her head so not to offend him further.

"Bracha, go fetch water," her mother said, and Bracha complied wordlessly. Her father was not a harsh man ordinarily, but times had been hard. He was a day laborer, and as he got older the younger men were hired first. It didn't help that some time back he had hurt his leg and it refused to heal properly. A day's work was hard to come by these days, and she knew it hurt his pride. Often the few pennies she brought from selling bread were what fed the family. She didn't blame Abba. She blamed the Romans. A Roman soldier had kicked her elderly father aside, breaking his leg badly and ruining his ability to provide for his family.

She took the water jar from beside the door and balanced it on one shoulder before making her way into the street toward a common well. There would be lines of women waiting, but today Bracha didn't mind. She wanted to be alone with her thoughts.

Benyamin had been worrying her lately. Her brother was going too far in his views, she knew. The things he talked about . . . the things he mentioned to her . . . they made her feel afraid. She felt like her brother was tipping over the edge of a well, and she couldn't move quickly enough to grab his tunic and pull him back. He was angry. So angry all the time. He kept pointing out sinners, his mouth twisting in a sneer as he spoke about their sins.

"That man walks a league every Sabbath!" he'd spit out.

"That woman is no better than a harlot! Do you see her bare head?" But the woman's head would not be bare. She would be struggling in the wind, sand blasting against her face as she tried to keep one strand from blowing free.

His anger, his judgment, his zeal was beginning to frighten her. And now there was the centurion who kept turning up, his steely eyes locked on her when she least expected it . . .

Bracha turned around with a shiver, scanning the faces behind her. No, he was not there. She was getting as jumpy as a wild goat. She sighed and tried to calm her breathing. What was happening to her?

". . . healed a blind man," she heard someone saying. "A *blind* man. I saw it! He looked right at me, and he could *see* me!"

"Who knows if he was really blind?" another asked.

"He was my brother!" came the quick reply.

"And he knew you when he saw you?"

"Of course not. But he did see me . . . and when I spoke, he knew my voice—"

"Yeshua did this?" someone questioned. "Yeshua—from Nazareth of all places?"

"Yes!"

"It was my brother!"

Confused questions and excited answers melted into the general noise of the street as Bracha passed by. She sidestepped a pile of manure and muttered her apologies when an old man bumped roughly into her.

Yeshua . . . She'd heard of him often recently. The stories kept getting bigger and bigger, almost unbelievably so, if it weren't for the eyewitnesses who swore to the stories on the Temple and sacrifice. They said that he loved children. That he fed people . . . hungry people. They said that he healed beggars, touched lepers, even raised dead men! The stories were amazing, and while there were many who brushed them off as the lengthening shadow of gossip, Bracha wanted to believe. She wanted the stories to be true. If there were a man like Yeshua . . . if there were a man who cared for children and healed women . . . if there were a man who had the power of Elohim, then her life in this squalor might not be so dismal after all. There would be hope. She did not know what she could possibly hope for, but there was hope that she would have hope, and that was something more than she had now.

If there were a man like Yeshua . . . dare she even think it?

Her brother insisted that the Messiah would be a fighter, a king. It was wicked to imagine that the Messiah might be otherwise. The men knew what the Torah said. Benyamin would know.

And while it might be wicked, she thought it would be so nice . . . so comforting . . . if the Messiah would be a little more like the Yeshua people kept talking about, from Nazareth.

Gaius Markus Africanus enjoyed chasing women. He enjoyed the pursuit. He enjoyed the feeling of power when a pretty face looked up at him in awe. He enjoyed the trouble of convincing the woman that he was desirable enough to take the risk. Gaius enjoyed pursuing women. He was a soldier after all. It was in his blood.

Gaius sat in a bar, his back to the wall, facing the door. It was habit, and in a place like that that catered to the military there weren't many men who sat easily with their backs to the door. It was a dim establishment that sold the usual varieties of drinks as well as some basic food fare. Gaius sat on a stool, his elbows resting on a wooden table rubbed smooth by countless forearms before his. A cup of spiced wine sat in front of him and he nodded a salutation to another officer who had just entered, the door banging behind him. Gaius' body hurt. Age seemed to be creeping up on him. His feet ached, his knees felt tight, and he desperately wanted a massage at a bathhouse, but was too tired to lift himself off the stool. "To Rome," he muttered blearily to himself, his words slurring a little. "May she never fail . . ." He raised the cup a hand span off the table, saluting no one in particular.

But she couldn't fail . . . not Rome. That was what was so glorious about her. Rome was invincible . . . indestructible . . . incapable of failure. Rome's armies could not be vanquished. The very thought brought tears to his eyes. Rome was beautiful. Logical. Rome had sprouted from the moral fiber of farmers who worked with their hands and loved her very soil. She was the jewel of the known world.

"I'm drunk." This was a quiet announcement to himself and it made him chuckle softly.

No, Rome's armies could not fail. From the moment a man entered the army, he knew that he had no choice but to succeed. A centurion's job was to impress upon the men under him the severity of Rome's expectations. A misstep brought a beating. Exhaustion brought a beating. Weakness, falsehood, and fear brought a beating. A soldier learned to obey first and think later. He learned to shout "Yes, sir!" and to slam his fist against his breastplate. He learned that death on the end of an enemy's sword was preferable to creative punishment at the hands at his centurion.

Failure was not an option for the soldiers under Gaius Markus African. Failure was not an option for him, either. A man had to trust the men under him. There were stories filtering through the legions about centurions who found themselves mysteriously alone in battle or a skirmish . . . as if their foot soldiers suddenly evaporated. More than one centurion had died leading his men into a fight. It was a dangerous profession, but it was more dangerous still if your men loathed you. A centurion walked a fine line between respect and hatred.

Gaius remembered his first taste of battle when he was only 16. He remembered marching in formation with his squadron, the sound of stamping feet and rattling armor drowning the thoughts out of his head. He remembered faltering only once, and feeling the sharp butt of a spear in his back, shoving him forward, keeping him moving. A boy no older than himself marched beside him, and when Gaius looked over at his companion he saw an ashen face and pure terror. The boy looked ready to soil himself. Gaius had the urge to encourage him, but he could not. A Roman army marched in dead, eerie silence toward her enemy. To break that silence was punishable by death.

The army of barbarians came running toward them in a screaming mass. They shook their swords and their painted faces leered from behind their helmets like faces of the dead from beyond the River. Gaius' blood ran cold, but still the signal had not come. They marched on . . . *stamp* . . . *stamp* . . . *stamp* . . . steadily forward, their faces immobile and their armor glinting dangerously in the sunlight.

And then the horn blew the long, long note, and Rome's battle cry erupted form the soldiers' throats. All of their pent up fear, anger, rage, and loathing exploded in a roar, and they broke into a run. Each cohort kept in formation, sprinting together toward the barbarians. They were trained to keep together . . . to fight together . . . to step over the bodies of the slain and keep on going forward until told to retreat. Rome never stopped . . . never faltered . . . never failed.

That was Gaius' first victory. It tasted of blood and sweat. He was exhausted, but elated. After what felt like hours of stabbing, hacking, chopping, and kicking writhing bodies off the end of his spear, it was over and he still breathed. To be alive was victory enough.

As he walked through the bodies, looking for loot, he could smell the blood and mud mixed together. He could hear the sweet chirp of birds. He could feel his heart pounding. And then he saw the boy who had marched next to him. He lay face up on the bloody ground. A ragged hole gaped in his neck, and his eyes were open. It was the open eyes that Gaius could never forget. He had seen death his entire lifetime, from the arenas and gladiators to punished soldiers who had fallen asleep at a post. But never before had a body affected Gaius as deeply as the body of the nameless boy. It was like looking into a mirror and seeing his own youth and vitality drained away from a ragged wound in his neck. Little did he know that his youth and vitality would leave him anyway, no matter how hard he tried to cling to them.

Gaius shook his head, pushing the memories back down where they belonged. When he was drunk and melancholy was no time to delve into past horrors. He wasn't that drunk. Instead, he recalled the beautiful Jewish girl, allowing his mind to wander over her various attributes . . . that stray curl . . . the slender forearms exposed as she tried to balance the load . . . those anxious, dark eyes that drew him in . . .

Yes, Gaius enjoyed chasing women. It was in his blood. It covered the memories he wanted to forget. It boiled his blood and made him feel young again. It filled his wine-hazed mind and pushed out everything else. All but the image of the beautiful Jewish girl.

CHAPTER 9

WOMAN TO WOMAN

Merav accepted the cup of goat's milk from her hostess and took a polite sip. Merav and Shahar were close to the same age. They'd grown up together in Yericho. Their fathers had been business associates and they had much opportunity to develop a cordial friendship. However, girls being the way girls can be, they had not.

"Welcome to my home," Shahar said sweetly. "It has been a long time since we have spoken to each other. I hope you are well."

Yes, Shahar would be gracious. Merav had never doubted she would have a warm reception. In the society of girls around the town, there was a hierarchy that had only marginally to do with their fathers' social positions. Each girl knew exactly which of them was the prettiest, and Shahar was always the prettiest. She had always been gracious, too. Merav wondered how gracious Shahar would have been if she had grown up with a face like her own.

"You have a beautiful home," Merav said, returning the smile. She folded her hands in her lap. "How is your husband?"

"Chayim is doing as well as I can keep him," came the chortled reply.

Yes, it was the answer of a woman with a husband who kept her well. Merav knew that Shahar had much to graciously deprecate.

"My son . . ." Shahar stopped, her voice choking. "Time does not make it easier, I'm afraid. But then, you lost a husband, and I'm sure you understand that."

Merav nodded.

"I have girls," she said. "All grown and married now. It's strange how our children become adults so quickly."

"Yes," Shahar sighed.

"I have come to speak with you about something quite delicate," Merav said slowly. "I won't disrespect you by wandering around the well."

Shahar's expression froze, then turned curious. She seated herself next to Merav and adjusted her robes to cover her ankles, then lifted her pretty face to look solemnly into Merav's.

"Go ahead," she said.

"I am widowed," Merav said. Her voice caught, and she cleared her throat. "I am not old, though. We are still vital women."

Shahar made a polite noise.

"I have some land adjoining your own," she said. "It is very profitable land, yet my nephew would like to arrange for my marriage to an old goat that would never be able to work with it."

"A marriage is something to rejoice about, however," Shahar pointed out carefully.

"It is," Merav admitted. "But this match is not to my liking. My nephew means well, but he only thinks of ridding himself of me, not of the rest of my life."

"You want to sell this land?"

"No," Merav said. "I would like to keep it. I would like to join it to your own."

"However would you do that?" Shahar asked, her pretty lips puckering in thought. "Land is joined through sale or by marriage."

Merav did not speak, allowing the woman to work it through for herself.

"You aren't suggesting you become the second wife!" Shahar snapped, her eyes suddenly filled with disgust and fury.

"No, no!" Merav broke in. "I would not suggest such a thing. You and I would never share a husband well, I am sure." She gave what she hoped was a reassuring smile. "Shahar, you have a peculiar situation on your hands."

"I do?" she asked primly.

Merav sighed. She was offending. That would never achieve her goal.

"Your remaining son is . . . a good man," Merav said slowly. "I feel that I understand him in many ways. He is indeed a man, Shahar. He is grown well past the age that would allow him to marry. I am younger than you are by several years, I should add. I do not point this out for stupid womanly quarrels, but to make a logical point."

"You wish to marry . . . Zacchaeus?" Shahar asked in shock.

"Finding a girl's family willing to marry her to Zacchaeus will be difficult at best," Merav said bluntly. "He is considered freakishly short. It is said that it is because of some horrible sin, and this rumor alone will make your son unmarriageable. To add to the difficulties, he is also a tax collector. No family will wish to make that alliance."

"But yours will?" Shahar had grown very pale. Her lips were almost white, but her eyes locked on Merav's face with a strange ferocity.

"The hardest part has been said," Merav said, softening her tone. "I know that it would be strange to have me as your daughter-in-law, but I would not be underfoot. I would work hard to further your son. I would defer to you. I could even live in a house away from you if you preferred. I would also give my plot of land into the hands of your son to do with as he saw fit. It would give wealth to your family. Considering the choice between myself, a woman old enough to be his mother, and a younger woman scraped off the street, I hope that I would be a preferable solution."

"You do not worry that I would find this repugnant?" Shahar asked, her voice low.

"I do worry about that," Merav admitted. "But a matter of 15 years is not a large matter. Marriages of this age differences have been made before for monetary purposes. Admittedly, I could not give your son children, but he would not have legitimate children if he were unmarried anyway. He could also take a second wife, if you decided it best. Perhaps a servant or a slave. She could be below me."

"And what would you give to Zacchaeus?" Shahar asked. "What of him?"

"We have become friends," Merav said. "I understand him. I feel his pain and I see why he does what he does. I could be a companion to him. I could be a support. I could be . . . an influence . . ."

"Suggesting what?" Shahar asked cautiously.

"A young wife can manipulate her husband with womanly wiles," Merav said. "But she would be more swayed by wealth, and he would not respect her opinion. A woman like myself, however, would be able to see your perspective very easily, and may be able to influence her husband to make certain decisions based on his respect for her."

Shahar was silent. She pursed her lips and clenched her jaw, her eyes staring at a point over Merav's shoulder. She finally exhaled and met Merav's eyes with a steady gaze.

"I see the value in what you propose," she said finally. "However, I am a woman. These decisions are not up to me."

Merav gave a slight nod. "No, they are not," she said. "But you are an intelligent woman, and a beautiful one. I have no doubt that your husband would hear you if you had a suggestion. I could only ask that you hear me, and the rest we must leave up to Adonai and the men."

Merav pushed herself to her feet, feeling her height against the petite form of Zacchaeus' mother. The smaller woman seemed to feel it, too, and she took a step away.

"May Adonai keep you, Shahar," she said sincerely.

"And you," Shahar murmured, her face clouded with thought.

And Merav walked away, as she knew she must. She had already done leagues more than she properly should have as a woman. Her nephew, and Zacchaeus, too, for that matter, had no idea whom they were dealing with.

CHAPTER 10

BETRAYAL

The summer heat was near its end. Zacchaeus could feel it. He could feel the first whiff of moisture in the air, the faintest prediction of the first rains to come. With the first rains came the plowing season when farmers tilled their fields in preparation to sow their crops. With the rains also came the festivals of Hashana and Yom Kippur. They were solemn times, times of reflection and repentance in the New Year. Just as the fields were prepared for sowing, so were Judeans prepared for the Day of Atonement.

Zacchaeus knew that he was not a righteous man, and this time of year always came with a niggling feeling of doubt and fear in the pit of his belly. He could not smell the rains to come without slight anxiety. If public opinion were correct, then he was steeped in sin since his conception. His freakishly short height, his choice to tax Adonai's people—Zacchaeus did not lie to himself. The city had decided for him. He was one of the wicked.

However, being publicly denounced as wicked was not a new experience for Zacchaeus. It did not change the fact that the summer heat was abating, the sun was shining, and there was the scent of rain in the air. While rain reminded him of the religious holidays to come, it also brought back memories of his boyhood with Oshri—happy memories of tree climbing and shared jokes.

The summer figs were ripe, ready to drop the fruit, and as Zacchaeus passed a fig tree he stopped to reach into the low hanging branches, plump, sticky figs plopping easily into his palm. They were syrupy and sweet, and as he looked up into the leaves with a bite of fig stuck into one cheek, he could have sworn he saw Oshri's young face laughing down at him. But when he blinked, the dream was gone, leaving only the rustling leaves, heavy fruit, and a sad smile on his face.

Today, however, Zacchaeus was going to the marketplace. He wanted a new robe and had decided to find some appropriate fabric himself. Truth be told, he liked to buy expensive things, not because he wanted the items so much as he wanted the basic interaction between himself and the merchants. Merchants had a reason to be nice to him. They smiled, thumped him on the shoulder, and called him "friend." It was all about the money. Zacchaeus was no fool, but all the same . . .

Yericho's streets were always crowded on market days and as Zacchaeus munched on the sticky figs, licking the juice off his hand and feeling the sugar between his fingers, he felt surprisingly cheerful. He felt like a boy again, enjoying a simple pleasure. The jostling of the crowd, the laughter of children playing in the street, the smell of fresh bread being sold by a pretty girl mixed with the scent of animal urine, strong spices, and sweat. There was something about the city that made a man feel alive! Wicked or not, he was in the mood to bargain . . .

The market spilled out of the busy square with merchants and their ware lining the streets that led up to the center of business. Zacchaeus declined to purchase "the sweetest melons of Yericho," passed by "the perfect gift for his beloved," and waved off a street urchin selling "good luck charms to keep off the evil eye." He smiled at the charms, for they were nothing but braided grass, and he was relatively certain that he'd survived more evil eyes than most of Yericho combined. His secret talisman was cold, hard coin.

The flowing sea of people was mostly strangers, or relative strangers to him, but there was one man, not far away, that he recognized immediately. He had seen that narrow face with the hooked nose his entire life, even while growing up. He'd watched the gray creep into the scraggly beard, and it was odd to see his cousin looking so . . . old. He stood in animated conversation with another man from their community.

He angled his steps in his cousin Yakov's direction, and as he got closer, the less he could see. People always obscured his view, and Zacchaeus muttered his insincere apologies as he pushed through the crowds, stepping harder than he needed to on some feet, but the old irritation kept rising up. He could hear his cousin's voice before he saw him.

". . . is a splendid cook. You've never tasted a goat as tender as my wife can cook!"

"Such a happy event, my friend. The birth of a son!"

"A handsome, strong boy!"

"Please, celebrate with us this evening," Yakov was saying. "At a time like this, joy is never full without a full house."

As Zacchaeus came into view of his cousin, he noticed the change in Yakov's expression. He cleared his throat and nodded several times, clapping his friend on the shoulder.

"Well here," Yakov said, clearing his throat.

The other man turned and looked at Zacchaeus. His expression also changed. He nodded several times and then excused himself.

"Yakov!" Zacchaeus said, a smile breaking over his face. "I hear congratulations are in order. A strong boy!"

"Yes, yes," Yakov nodded accepting the congratulations with a less enthusiastic smile. "Praise Adonai. I am thankful, indeed."

Zacchaeus stood watching his cousin's squirms of discomfort. While Yakov had always been a self-righteous mouse, Zacchaeus felt sincere happiness for his cousin rising up inside of him. A boy was the wish of every new father . . . a boy and a safe delivery. It seemed that his cousin had received both.

"I am truly happy for you and your beautiful wife," Zacchaeus said, holding out his hands. He let them drop when Yakov made no move to reciprocate the gesture. Zacchaeus' spontaneous happiness for his cousin was quickly evaporating, and he resented the small untruth he told about Yakov's wife being beautiful. She had teeth like a camel, skin like a snake, and the posture of an old mule. She was a sight, certainly . . . but she'd come with money and a father with position. Zacchaeus remembered cringing at the wedding feast, pitying the poor children to be born to such awkward parents.

"Thank you," Yakov said, his voice wooden. "May Elohim be with you, cousin."

"Are you off so soon?" Zacchaeus asked. "Are you busy preparing for a feast, perhaps?"

"A feast?" Yakov let out a wheezing laugh. "A feast?"

"It would be customary to celebrate the arrival of your son, would it not?" Zacchaeus asked, looking with practiced sincerity into his cousin's nervous face.

"A small dinner . . . nothing big . . . a few friends whom I owe. Nothing much . . ." Yakov stammered, his voice trailing away.

"Then I'm sure you would welcome family who would support you with joy," Zacchaeus said.

"My dear cousin," Yakov said, swallowing quickly. "Let me invite you to my home when I am better prepared to serve you in the manner you deserve. I cannot ask you to come to such a humble, small gathering as this. I will certainly invite you very soon, when all will be prepared to honor you."

"Of course," Zacchaeus said, stepping back. He'd toyed with his cousin long enough. He knew he would never be welcome in Yakov's home, but some part of him enjoyed pushing the little man to his limit of nervous tension. "Please tell your wife how happy I am for your new son."

Yakov sighed in unveiled relief and awkwardly jabbed his fingers at Zacchaeus' shoulder in a gesture of farewell before skittering off into the crowd.

A roasted goat, apparently, was not elevated enough for the likes of Zacchaeus. He spat on the ground and shook his head.

"May the poor boy have better looks than his mother and more brains than his father," he muttered. It was the kindest thing he could think to say.

As Zacchaeus walked in the direction of the sycamore tree, seeking shade, he looked up at the gnarled, twisting branches, and his mind returned to the years of boyhood. There was something about climbing a tree that made a boy feel like he owned the world. And there was something about a tree that made Zacchaeus yearn to climb up into it and be a boy again . . . a boy with a brother by his side.

Ehud noticed how much he wanted to spend some coin just when it was impossible for him to do so. He had never enjoyed looking at veils, necklaces, or earrings for his wife. It was all just a jumble of cloth and beads to him . . . something best left to the womenfolk. But now that he knew he could not spend, not even to buy a trinket for luck, the blankets spread out to display combs and veils seemed to draw him like a sheep to grass. The booths with pottery, kettles, and pokers seemed unimaginably desirable. Sealed jars of oil seemed to taunt him from a cart.

Borrowing money had seemed too easy when he looked back on it. The moneylender was so eager to please him. He had believed in Ehud's vision. He had explained that the high interest rate was just a precaution, but that Ehud's plan for a vineyard was sure to be a success. In fact, it shouldn't have been too terribly expensive to start, but his family had disagreed with him.

"No, son," his father had said. "There is a good winery in Yericho, and it takes too long to perfect a wineskin of wine. Either you open it too early, or too late. It's best to stay with the family business."

"No, brother," his brother had said. "You insult our father with this foolishness. We weave. It is what we do. I will not help you in this."

But the moneylender had seen Ehud's dream . . . he had seen the fortune that Ehud would make for his family as solidly as Ehud had. In fact, Ehud hadn't even needed to borrow very much money. The principal was relatively small, but the longer it took for Ehud to repay, and the more that went wrong with his fledgling business, the faster that little lump of debt grew, the interest compounding like ants pouring out of a hole in the ground, until the debt was too massive to ever repay.

Ehud had never been wise with money. He took after his mother, unfortunately. His father had been a solid businessman, weaving intricate fabrics and selling them to the wealthiest of families. Ehud should have been proud to work with his father the way his older brothers had been, but he had always harbored shame for the trade. Weaving was women's work, and he could not ignore the stigma.

Ehud's mother used to sell her baking, always intending to make a profit. Unfortunately, she had a woman's head for business and did not understand how profits came about. She would spend money on expensive ingredients, highest quality oil, and beautifully worked kitchen utensils. It was for the business, she always explained, and his father had amused her. Then she would go out to sell the bread she baked. Most of it would be given away to friends or poor people. What little she did sell, she sold at a deep discount out of a desire not to appear to need the money. It all ended up as a very expensive hobby that amused Ehud's mother for many years.

Ehud, as he looked around the marketplace, wondered dismally if he had a woman's head for business, after all. If anyone would have suggested such an insult before this, he would have fought him on the spot, defending his honor. However, Ehud could not deny the facts. Given a small amount of money to start a business, he had lost

almost all of it. The small portion of a vineyard he purchased pro-
duced very few and very sour grapes. Even after trodding out the
juice in a bedrock basin, he was unpracticed in the care of wineskins
and several burst. He did not know the exact moment that the wine
was perfect, or how to properly protect it from too much heat. The
protective cave he dug to shield the wine from the late summer heat
was not sufficient, but he did not know this until it was too late. His
trial and error method had been more expensive that he'd thought.
Two wineskins had turned out very nicely, and he had drunk them
with his family, enjoying them immensely. He knew that he could
make good wine. He knew it! But the next wineskins that he had
opened were foul, and he wasn't sure what had gone wrong. He
had not one saleable drop of wine, and he had one suddenly very
unfriendly moneylender with his hand out.

"What will we do?" his wife had asked.

"Don't worry your pretty head over money, wife," he had said.
"Have I not cared for you this many years?"

"Father?" his daughter had whispered. "Are we poor now?"

"Nonsense!" he'd laughed. "My dear, sweet girl . . . I am your
father. This is business, and women cannot understand it. Please
don't worry yourself over it. I am taking care of everything."

And so they had trusted him. His wife did not ask him about it
again, and his daughter seemed quite content to trust her father to
provide a happy life for her. Of course, the women did not question
him. He was the man of the house and master of their futures. He
did not expect anything less, but the weight of his responsibility
hung heavy over him. He knew how much he had to repay, and did
not know how to do it.

Ehud had sat up late into the night. He had sat in the dark, the
lamp having long ago sputtered out leaving a soft coiling wisp of
smoke barely visible in the moonlight. He had sat that way for a long
time, listening to the dogs bark and night birds call. He had sat that
way, his breath coming in shallow gasps. He owed more money than
he could ever repay. He did not know what to do.

"Oh, Elohim! God of my fathers," he had prayed. "Work a miracle for me. Give me the money that I need so that I can be pulled
out of this pit."

But so far, Elohim had not answered. He was as silent and dis-
tant as the moneylender. The heavens seemed to throw his prayers

back down to the earth, and sleep became impossible. He sat up every night, staring into the darkness. His eyes stung with exhaustion, but he could not sleep more than a couple of hours each night, finally dropping into a fitful, nightmare plagued slumber.

"Husband," his wife whispered one night. "You are in pain. May I help you?"

He shook his head.

"Husband," she had said after a few moments. "I do not care if we lose our money. I would live with you in a hole. Adonai will provide. Please, come to bed and rest."

But God had not provided, and going to bed to rest was as impossible as repaying the debt. So he sat awake at night, staring into the darkness, his heart heavy. He wished he could lie down and die, but he could not leave this burden to his wife and one unmarried daughter. He was the man and this burden belonged on his shoulders.

One night, after the lamp had sputtered out, he sat in miserable silence in his home. It was this night that he overheard some whispers outside. He crept to the window and listened. It was his neighbor discussing an inheritance with his brother. The inheritance would give them a large plot of land in a neighboring community . . . No one would know about it. They were planning to hide the information from the Roman authorities to spare themselves the crippling taxes. For the first time in a long time, Ehud felt a swell of power. For the first time in a long time, Ehud saw an escape.

So now, as Ehud stood in the market, he was not looking for a bargain on doves or a trinket for his wife. Ehud was looking for someone in particular . . . a man interested in the information that he gleaned from his neighbors . . .

"Zacchaeus," Ehud said, keeping his voice low. The small man turned, raised his eyes up to look him in the face, and cast him a questioning look.

"Ehud?" Zacchaeus said it like a question.

"Please, sir," Ehud whispered. "I can't be seen speaking with you."

Zacchaeus walked away, and Ehud knew what was expected of him. He followed the little man at a distance as he meandered through the market then dodged after him into a narrow alley, out of sight. Ehud's heart was pounding and while he knew that no one could see him, he kept casting furtive glances over his shoulder to be sure.

Strewn through the alley was some broken pottery, a cracked pot leaking filthy water, the stink of excrement, some dried brush, and the slippery, pungent remnants of rotting garbage. Zacchaeus turned up his nose delicately and covered his mouth with one hand, rings glittering in the dim, dusty light.

"You have something for me?" Zacchaeus asked, his voice low.

"What is it worth?" Ehud asked.

"Coin, I'm sure," Zacchaeus replied with an amused look. "How much coin depends on the information."

"My brother-in-law, Abram, acquired a field adjacent to his," Zacchaeus said. "He did not spend much for it, since the family was pressed for money and would take anything he offered, but it is worth far more than he paid."

"This is interesting," Zacchaeus said, nodding. "I like it. What else?"

"The tanner's cousin died several months ago, and he found out recently that he was left some money . . . I couldn't discover how much, though. I tried."

"What else?" Zacchaeus pushed.

Ehud clenched his teeth in anger. He hated this. He hated reporting on his own people. He hated cringing before this freakish little man, scraping for some coins. Zacchaeus' eyes were pinned on Ehud' face and his mouth broke into a broad smile, a soft chuckle coming out of the shorter man's chest.

"I amuse you?" Ehud snapped.

"Very much," Zacchaeus replied. "Go on, what else do you have?"

"Nothing." Ehud let his gaze go down to the ground, watching a rat that scampered past them, squeezed itself into a hole, and disappeared.

"Don't feel so badly, Ehud," Zacchaeus said, his voice softening. "They can afford to pay. They may not like it, mind you, but they can afford it."

As Ehud's eyes came back up to the face of the tax collector, he saw genuine sympathy in the little man's eyes.

"Take the money, Ehud," Zacchaeus said firmly. "You've earned it."

Ehud felt the coins pressed into his palm, and closed his fingers over them. He was silent, smelling the filth around him and hating himself for his betrayal of his neighbors and family.

"Care for yourself, friend," Zacchaeus said softly as he pushed past and back into the sunlight. "No one else will."

CHAPTER 11

Afraid

Benyamin's stomach felt tight and his throat was constricted. He clamped his lips shut and breathed heavily through his nose as he strode through the busy streets of Yericho. He had once again failed to be hired for the day, but this was not the cause of his tension. His stomach always felt tight and his throat was always constricted. In fact, Benyamin thought that he was quite relaxed.

As he walked, he prayed. Benyamin prayed while he did everything. He prayed while he worked. He prayed while he ate. He prayed while he lay on his thin little mat, looking up at the ceiling of his father's house. Benyamin was a righteous man. He was a devoted man. He was a praying man.

By the rivers of Babylon we sat and wept when we remembered Zion . . .

The words were a song of David and they spilled through his mind with the ease of a river spilling through its bed. The words were familiar and sad.

There on the poplars we hung our harps, for there our captors asked us for songs, our tormentors demanded songs of joy; and they said, "Sing us one of the songs of Zion."

The song of David had a melancholy, lilting melody, and his voice was hoarse with emotion as he hummed the tune in time to his steps.

By the rivers of Babylon, we sat and wept . . .

Benyamin felt a lump in his throat as the words meandered through his mind. He understood the anguish of Israelite prisoners. He understood how they would have longed to see their home once more. But if they'd returned home to Yerushalayim to see it occupied by Roman pigs, they would have laid down their harps once more and wept for what dear Yerushalayim had become.

How can we sing the songs of Adonai while in a foreign land? If I forget you, O Yerushalayim . . .

If Benyamin forgot her, may his right hand forget its skill . . .

may his tongue cleave to the roof of his mouth if he did not remember. He loved Yerushalayim. He loved her walls, her towers, her streets, and temple. He loved the smell of her, the feeling of her beneath his feet. He adored dear Yerushalayim. He adored this rocky, beautiful land of the Lord.

Yet, in his very sight, like a man forced to see his wife raped, he had to watch sweet Yerushalayim ravished by pagan dogs. The very thought twisted his lips in disgust and brought tears of anguish to his eyes. They blurred his vision. He felt a shuddering sadness descend upon his chest and he struggled to control his emotions.

"O Daughter of Babylon . . . happy is he who repays you for what you have done to us." He sung the words softly, his voice tense with restricted emotion. "Happy is he who seizes your infants and dashes them against the rocks."

Yes! The thought of the babies being killed against the rocks gave him a surge of elation. It was a righteous elation, he thought. It was an elation brought by devotion to Elohim. He wiped at a tear that had trickled down his cheek, then darted an angry look at a boy who was staring at him, his eyes wide. He hated drawing attention to himself. He hated that love for Yerushalayim was so strange in these wicked days that tears of devotion would draw stares. He hated it all.

The streets of Yericho were bustling this afternoon. He was hungry. All morning, and most of the afternoon waiting to be hired for a day's work left a man empty. Yet Elohim was king of the universe, and if Elohim did not give the work, then there was a reason. Benyamin was not a man created for mundane labor. He had been born to defend Elohim's wishes, to fight for dear Yerushalayim. Benyamin would not lay down his harp and weep for long. He would take up his sword and fight.

As Benyamin walked, his mind followed familiar pathways. He thought of Rome and her cruel, evil rule. He thought of the occupation, defiling the land with the filthy touch of the Roman pigs. He thought of the Judean women and their fall from modest discretion. He saw flashes of forearms, exposed ankles, lengths of tender neck, tendrils of hair escaping the proper covering . . . all designed to enflame a man's senses so that he could think of nothing else. Jewish women, women of God, were slipping into the harlotry of the Romans! He struggled to shove the sensual images from his mind, whispering a prayer of piety and guilt.

Benyamin's stomach felt tight and his throat was constricted. He breathed deeply through his nose and let his eyes scan the crowds of people. He did not like to be caught unawares and was always nervous that someone might recognize him, shaking an accusing finger in his direction. He scanned the crowds, his dark eyes fearlessly moving from face to face until he stopped on one face in particular. A small smile came to his lips at the sight of his sister, Bracha.

He had older sisters who were already married and an older brother who had been killed in an accident during a job, but Bracha had always been his favorite. Seven years her senior, he felt a certain protectiveness toward her. She was more beautiful than she realized. His family had been careful not to fill her mind with vanity, and had never complimented her on her appearance. Not once. He regularly called her plain and dull so that she would not be caught in a web of conceit. But she was anything but plain. She was anything but dull. She was radiant and lovely. He was proud that she was his own sister.

"Bracha!" he called, and raised a hand. She turned in his direction and gave a small smile when she saw him. Yes, she was a good young woman, not ever showing too much emotion as was proper. She turned in his direction, and as she did, he saw something that chilled him.

Standing not far away, his eyes pinned to his sister like a Sabbath handkerchief, was a centurion. He was tall, strong, and animalistic. His eyes, steely and intent, roved up and down his sister's robed length. His lips were pursed in admiration and his head was cocked at an appraising angle. The sight of that pig eyeing his sister like a piece of horseflesh made his skin crawl. Benyamin's eyes narrowed in loathing and he clenched his jaw, grinding sand between his teeth.

Benyamin knew, however, that while his hatred was strong, his strength was not in a face-to-face attack. He was wiry. He was quick, but he was also half the size of that monster. He was not armed. He was not defended. He would writhe on the end of that brute's spear and die for nothing. Benyamin knew his strengths, but he also knew his weaknesses. It was his weakness that he hated most.

"You!" he snapped and Bracha eyed him warily.

"Brother," she said, her voice quiet.

"You!" he repeated. "What have you done?"

"Nothing," she said, shaking her head. "I've sold my bread."

"Drawing the eyes of Roman pigs, is what you're doing," he hissed. He looked back in the direction of the centurion and saw those narrowed, hawk-like eyes focused on them, giving him a shiver of fear.

"What?" she asked, about to look around in confusion. Benyamin grabbed her soft arm and squeezed hard, enjoying her yelp of surprise.

"Are you looking for your admirer?" he asked in disgust.

Bracha stared at him in frightened silence, her eyes darting around him as if trying to find something to latch on to that might give her answers.

"You're a tramp!" he spat. "A no good harlot, no better than the Roman filth that wander these streets! Cover yourself, you ugly mutt. Cover yourself!"

Bracha struggled to pull her veil closer over her face, her eyes staring at him, wide and shaken. She pulled her hands into her robes and clutched at the fabric from the inside, trying to cover every bit of skin she could.

"I didn't know," she whispered. "Benyamin, I didn't know. I'm sorry."

"A woman should remain silent in public!" he shouted, his voice rising in fury. "Silent!"

She stopped her frantic whispers and ducked her head instead. Benyamin felt a surge of manly strength that made him feel bigger than his diminutive frame and stronger than his wiry muscles. He looked at his sister, silently daring her to say another word, but she would not look up and kept herself covered. He nodded to himself in satisfaction.

What Benyamin did not see was that the centurion's steely gaze had moved from young Bracha to her domineering brother.

And he was memorizing Benyamin's face.

Tzofit lay alone on her bed. She was still not accustomed to this. During her womanly time of the month she was used to sleeping on a mat in a different room, but to be lying alone in the bed she normally shared with Oshri was strange. It was strange not to feel the heat of his arm next to hers. It was strange not to hear his snores. It was strange not to have to lie perfectly still so she wouldn't waken him while she stared out into the night. She could move freely if she wanted to, but she still lay on her side of the bed, perfectly still.

While Tzofit had thought of her husband as little as possible during his life, now that he had died, her memories of him were confusingly strong. She felt like she could see him in crowds, could smell him in an empty room, or hear his voice in the clatter of cooking.

Tzofit's parents had chosen him because of his fine family. Tzofit's father-in-law had chosen her because of his business relationship to her father, and also because Tzofit was known to be a fine looking girl. Every man wanted to give his son a beautiful wife. Tzofit, after a long and elaborate wedding dinner, had experienced her first few moments alone with her new husband. She remembered standing before him in the honeymoon room that he had built onto his father's house, her veil still covering her hair.

"Let me see your hair," he said.

She blushed and allowed the veil to fall away, exposing her glossy black waves. She kept her eyes lowered. She knew what was expected of her. She felt shy and a little embarrassed to be looked at this way by a man who was not her blood relative. She felt the heat rising in her cheeks and she hurriedly pulled the veil back over her hair.

"Tzofit," he said quietly. "My wife."

"Yes," she said simply.

"My mother said that I should tell you how I like my clothes cared for," he said. "She said that I should explain it all to you early."

"Of course," she murmured, confused. Her mother had explained what would be expected of her on her wedding night, but she had not included household explanations in the description.

"How silly of me," he said, suddenly shaking his head and giving her a charming smile. "I have ordered some refreshments for us. Mother recommended something light, especially after all we've eaten."

She'd been too naïve to see it then, but her husband was still a boy in many ways and would remain so. She had no longing for her husband's love. She knew that parents loved their children, and that she would love her own children, too. She knew that if she had a son, he would be her greatest ally in this new family of in-laws. A baby, she knew, was the answer.

However, a baby was not forthcoming. The more time that passed without signs of pregnancy, the more miserable Tzofit became. Her husband discussed the subject at great length with his mother. Tzofit tried to talk to him in the dark hours when they lay together on their bed, whispering her apologies for remaining childless. She looked into his face, trying to see some sympathy in his shadowed expressions. She drank the foul tasting concoctions her mother-in-law gravely served her, hoping that they would work. She ducked her head and worked hard, praying, praying, *praying* that God would grant her a baby to end this constant, unending judgment.

The years passed, but there was no child. Her mother-in-law stopped giving her foul tasting concoctions. Her husband stopped hopefully eying her belly. And Tzofit seemed to slowly disappear into the sweaty kneading of unbaked bread, into the finger numbing repetition of the loom, and into the constant chopping, sweeping, arranging, cooking, and serving that fell to a woman.

Now as she lay in bed alone, it was easy to imagine that this was just another night when her husband had slipped out of their bed and gone to talk with his mother. It was nights just like this one that the anger and resentment pushed so hard against her chest that she thought she could not possibly take another breath. On nights like this one she had lain in bed, alone for the first time all day, remembering every slight, every insult, every implication . . . remembering, remembering, remembering . . . All her humiliation, rage, heartbreak, and anxiety sealed away inside of her like wine in a goatskin bag.

And like wine in a wineskin, one day Tzofit sprung a leak. It was not a big leak, more like a tiny spray of wine shooting out into the air. It was entirely unexpected and Tzofit had been shocked at herself.

Tzofit and Shahar were serving the evening meal, uncovering the dishes and arranging the flatbread. The family had gathered and the men were talking among themselves.

"Oshri," Shahar said, her voice becoming tender the way it always did when she addressed her eldest son. "You should eat more. You are getting thin."

"Oh, Mother," he said, waving away her worries with one hand. "I eat. I'm busy. You wouldn't understand."

She clucked her tongue and shook her head.

"Tzofit should be taking better care of you," she sighed.

"I would," Tzofit suddenly snapped, "if you would take the man off your hip!"

The room dropped into stony silence, and Tzofit stared down at the table full of men staring at her in shock. She gave a thin, cold smile in an attempt to mask her own dismay, and turned and left the room. As soon as she was out of sight, Tzofit sank to her knees, her teeth chattering in terror. They would beat her. They would starve her. She had done something horrible, and she hadn't been able to stop herself. Where had that come from? Her hands were clapped over her mouth as she tried to understand what she had just done.

"Oshri is a bit of baby still," she overheard Zacchaeus chuckle.

"He isn't!" Shahar snapped. "Don't speak of your brother that way!"

And the rest of the conversation lowered into inaudible tones . . . tones that Tzofit was sure were plotting her punishment.

Her punishment did come. It came in the form of more work, but no one ever said anything about what she had said, least of all her husband. And though she swore to herself that she would never make such a mistake again, it was like the small spraying leak kept getting larger and larger until the anger and spite poured out of her in a steady dribble. Dishes were deposited with more force than necessary. Wine was poured less carefully than was entirely polite. She bit her tongue, thinking of savage retorts she longed to sling back at the members of her husband's family.

Now as Tzofit lay in the bed she used to share with Oshri, she stared at the small window, her stomach tight with tension. She was no longer Oshri's wife. She was Oshri's widow. Her power was gone, if she ever could have claimed to have any. She was a child-less burden. She was a problem to be dealt with. She was a widow to be disposed of. And the people responsible for disposing of her had hated her for a long, long time.

Tzofit had reason to be afraid.

CHAPTER 12

The Outcasts

Ehud stood before the house of Seth, the moneylender, his heart beating almost audibly in his chest. He took a shaky breath and smoothed one hand over his beard. He had been appeased, hadn't he? He had seemed appeased . . . or had he? He had said that Ehud could have a little more time. He had taken the coins that Ehud had proffered without counting them. They had passed the point of Ehud even demanding a receipt or a witness. The debt was staggering, and the few coins would only appease Seth for a short time.

Yericho's streets were in a lull, the dipping of the sun and the time for the evening meal calling most people home. The smell of cooking fires, seared meat, sizzling spices, dust, sweat, and dung mingled together in one comforting aroma. It was the smell of the city that usually made Ehud's feet angle themselves toward home with his stomach rumbling and his mind fixed on whatever meal his wife would have prepared for him. The smoke from cooking fires hung low over the city, in some areas thick enough to make his eyes water, but Ehud's mind was not on the meal that his wife, Dassah, was likely putting on the table. It was on the cost of the meal's ingredients that his wife was unknowingly wasting. It was on the debt that kept growing and growing despite his struggle to pay it. It was on the fickle moneylender, his overly curious neighbors, and his stubbornly trusting wife who stupidly took him at his word that all was well and she need not moderate her consumption in any way.

Ehud headed in the direction of his home, his eyes on the cobbled road ahead of him. He stepped over some horse manure, lifting his robe as he did so. The uneven stones of the street pressed through the leather soles of his sandals, making the bottoms of his feet ache. He glanced up at the rhythmic clunking of a wagon, pulled by a donkey, passing by. As he looked up, he saw one of his neighbors also walking in the homeward direction.

It was strange that seeing neighbors brought a nervous twitch to his lips now. He used to feel happy at the sight of an old friend, but times had changed. Not only was he hiding a crushing debt and financial collapse, not only was he trying desperately to keep his appearance strong and confident, but he was also fishing. It was what he was reduced to . . . fishing for information about his neighbors that he could report for a little more money.

"Aviram!" Ehud called, and when the man turned, he forced a smile to his face and gave what he hoped was a friendly wave.

Aviram was a burly man with a long black beard and shoulders as broad as an ox. He carried a load on his back, obviously having stopped by the market for some goods. He was a potter by trade, and good at his profession. His father had taught him well and he was known to be skilled. Ehud glanced appraisingly at the pack Aviram carried. He was obviously able to spend some coin without worry, Ehud noticed.

"Elohim be praised!" Aviram said with a booming laugh. "It is good to see a friend."

"It is," Ehud agreed with a wide smile. "A long walk home with an empty stomach can feel shorter with some good company."

"Ah . . ." Aviram laid a heavy hand on Ehud's shoulder and gave him a friendly shake that rattled Ehud's teeth. He walked on in contented silence.

"Your business is doing well," Ehud said.

"Moderately," Aviram said. "Elohim be praised."

"Oh, more than moderately," Ehud pressed. "Look at you! Fat with your beautiful wife's good cooking, smiling like a man with a new son."

"No new sons, my friend," Aviram said, shaking his head. "But Elohim has blessed us . . . blessed us indeed."

"A large contract?" Ehud asked. "Perhaps a large inheritance?"

Aviram gave Ehud a sideways look and frowned.

"So many questions, my friend," he said, his voice sounding more cautious.

"I am only wanting to share in a neighbor's joy," Ehud said, waving his hand dismissively. "It's been a long time since I've had my own good fortune . . ."

"Business is not doing well?" Aviram asked, his frown turning into a look of empathy.

"No, no . . ." Ehud sighed. This was not the direction he

wanted the conversation to take. "The business is doing as well as it can. I had hoped for another business possibility, but . . . well."

"Elohim blesses those who follow in their father's footsteps, friend," Aviram said, slapping Ehud on the back enthusiastically. "You are a good man, Ehud, a good man."

Ehud forced a smile in return, guilt seeping into his bones. He hated this. He hated picking at his friends for information. He hated reporting their good fortune to the Romans for a few extra coins. If he kept the extra money, he would be well off, indeed, but instead it was cast into the bottomless pit of Seth's coffers.

"You are doing well, though," Ehud said, gesturing toward the pack his friend carried.

Aviram gave Ehud a strange look, but kept his mouth shut. He suspected something. Ehud felt his stomach tighten in fear. Aviram suspected something.

It was only a matter of time, and Ehud knew it. Only a matter of time.

The evening meal had been cleared away, and Zacchaeus stood in his home. *His* home. Not his father's home. Not the home he was now heir to where his mother and father were going about their evening routines. It was strange. Years ago, when Zacchaeus had begun to put together his own home away from the pressures of his parents, brother, and sister-in-law, he had felt cheated out of the family home that had meant so much to him. Now, as a grown man entitled to that house, he was escaping again, back to this house that he had put together for himself.

Zacchaeus had always thought that his memories at his childhood home were the strongest, most precious memories he had. Yet tonight felt different. Tonight, after weeks of close quarters with his parents and sister-in-law, he felt relieved to be home. The courtyard with the potted shrubs, the walls enshrouded in elaborate tapestries, the low table surrounded with exotic pillows, the office, his desk covered in scrolls, quills, and pots of ink at various levels of use. This was the home that had become Zacchaeus' temple . . . his private, sacred space. His servants knew his quirks and anticipated his wants admirably.

Zacchaeus sat in a chair beside his bed, a basin of water before him. He splashed his face and rubbed at his cheeks vigorously. He blew out through his mouth, spraying water in front of him, then splashed water on his face again. Reaching blindly for a cloth, he found it and pressed it against his face.

Several lamps burned around the room, shedding their flickering, warm light. Being a tax collector had made Zacchaeus a wealthy man, but as heir to his father's fortune he was now wealthier still. Money did things in Yericho. Money eased the way for many, many difficulties. He was not liked or respected, but he was wealthy. Now, with his father's respectable fortune underneath him, Zacchaeus wondered what possibilities lay ahead.

What was life without a family? What was a home without guests? Yet somehow Zacchaeus had made do. He had lived independently, away from his kin. He had lovingly created a home that saw no guests and catered to one man only.

He smoothed his tunic over his chest and sat down on the edge of his bed. It was constructed out of elaborately carved olive wood and sat low to the ground as did all his furniture. The mattress was stuffed with feathers and layers of straw, topped by a thick fabric that stopped any uncomfortable pokes. The bed was comfortably layered with soft, light blankets that varied in color from bleached white to dark crimson, and he lay back staring up at the ceiling.

As a young man he used to dream of the dinner parties he would give. He would mentally plan each course of the meal, the layout of the lamps, the entertainment. He would imagine the gracious hospitality he would bestow upon his guests, and he would create wonderful, glowing reports of his dinner parties.

"The food was exquisite," someone would sigh. "I've never tasted dishes so divine. My belly was filled, but I never wanted to stop putting morsel after morsel between my lips."

"The courtyard was lit by a hundred lamps, all dancing and glowing in the moonlight," another guest would describe. "Zacchaeus spoke to each one of us, clasping our hands and laughing with us individually over memories we shared. I have never felt more at home or more delightfully happy than I did in the home of my dear friend."

Zacchaeus still enjoyed these fantasies. As he lay back on his bed, his eyes were shut and his lips moved in imagined conversation with imagined guests. His hands twitched in subdued gestures, and he smiled in relaxed satisfaction. After a few moments, his eyes fluttered open and he let out a long sigh.

It was not real. He was an outcast in more ways than he could control. No one wanted to eat at his home. No one wanted to enjoy his food or laugh in his company. There would be no admiring glances at the impeccable taste he displayed around his home. There would be no compliments on his choice of dishes that complimented each other as well as the wine. Yet he still held out hope that by becoming his father's heir, by accumulating more wealth to his name, then people would be willing to socialize with him, people would be willing to ignore his status and his deformity for the sake of being near his money. He held out hope that enough money would entice people to hide their true opinions and pretend to be his friends.

There was one woman who had desired his company. The thought made him frown. He did not fully understand Merav, but he found himself liking her. He liked her deep laugh. He liked her confident gaze and her eyes that spoke of years of experience that had failed to embitter her. He liked her quick wit. He found himself enjoying the memories of their last visit and realized that she was the perfect guest . . . the guest of fantasies.

Was it wrong to enjoy a flirtation with a much older woman? Obviously nothing could ever come of it, but it made him feel alive again . . . made him feel like there was still some excitement and enjoyment left in life.

If it were not so late tonight, he would send word and ask her to visit. He would tell the cook to prepare a light but enticing meal . . . he would begin to light the 100 lamps that would flicker and dance in the moonlight. If it were not so late tonight, he would laugh with her over excellent wine and listen to her talk about people he did not know.

But it was late. And tomorrow, in the light of the morning sun flooding through his bedroom window, he would not have the courage to send the invitation. It would not seem possible. It would not seem real.

Yet tonight, Zacchaeus lay on his back across his bed, his eyes shut and his lips moving in imagined conversation with the widow Merav.

Across the city of Yericho, across the meandering, crisscrossing streets . . . across the housetops, the windows lit from within . . . across the huddled forms of homeless people, genderless and faceless in the deepening shadows of Yericho's bowels . . . across the walls that enclosed the old city from the new, a different house butted up against the military base that declared Yericho "occupied." It was a Roman house, wealthy and respectable. It was guarded well, soldiers passing silently in front of the house front, stopping to talk quietly together and spit into the street before their eyes lifted again, scanning the shadows for dangerous design.

Inside this house, reclining on a low couch with a cup of watered wine in one hand, was Gaius Markus Africanus, centurion of the fourth cohort of the seventy-second legion. Having dismissed the servants from his presence, he sat alone. His wife and children were already retired. His eyes felt bleary from the effect of the wine but he was not ready to take himself to bed.

Today was the first anniversary of his father's death. While he had never been close to his father and, in fact, had some very bitter memories of the man, he could not help but feel the pain any child feels at the loss of a parent. While his father had been a brutal disciplinarian and a disinterested husband, he had been his father. Gaius had looked to him to see what a man should be. He had looked to him to see how he measured up, and when he saw that he did not, he loathed himself for his failure. He could never loathe his father. At least he could not admit such feelings to himself.

Tonight, instead of remembering his father's last days, Gaius' mind was traveling back to early boyhood.

Every boy had to face the day when he was taken from his mother's lap. Gaius remembered that day vividly, more vividly than one would imagine a grown man would remember a single day in his childhood. He remembered the feeling of his mother's hands on his cheeks, the smell of her hair as she bent over him, the sound of her voice as she kissed his forehead and said, "Today, son, your father has ordered that you will go out with him. You will visit the arena."

Gaius had stared at her mutely, terror rising up in his small chest. He did not know his father well, and what he did know of his father was made of discipline and harsh commands. He did not want to leave his mother's side. He did not want to leave the comfort of his home and go out with his father into the busy, bustling street.

Gaius, however, had not had a choice. His father had decided that today was the day that the boy would be introduced to some proper entertainment. It was time for Gaius to see what Romans paid good money to watch and place bets on. It was to be a wonderful show—each fight a fight to the death. Gladiators would face chariots and nets, hand to hand combat, even battles without weapons. They would face lions and bulls, and blood would bath the arena from morning till night. The roar of the crowd would be deafening, the smell of spilled wine would make Gaius want to vomit, and the sight of the gore would be seared into his mind for the rest of his life.

Gaius did not remember the trip back home afterward. He recalled short parts of conversation where his father recapped the carnage in terms of betting odds. And he remembered crawling into his bed, ashen and strangely calm.

"Gaius?" the gentle voice of his pedagogue asked.

Gaius turned over in his bed to face the slender man standing in his room. He stood with his hands folded in front of him like he was getting ready to pontificate on some scholarly subject, but he was silent, looking at the boy expectantly.

"Yes?" Gaius said.

"Did you have a nice time with your father?" the pedagogue asked.

Gaius was silent, unsure of how to answer, or even what the question meant.

"Ah," the young man said after a moment. "I think I understand."

"What?" asked Gaius, his voice trembling. "What do you understand?"

"You were at the arena for the first time," he said gently. "And that can be very hard for a boy."

"It was terrible," Gaius whispered. "Terrible! There was the blood . . . and the men cried out . . . and then more blood—"

He had no words to describe what he had seen. He had not known how to think about it.

"They were criminals," his teacher said in explanation. "They broke the law, and their punishment was death."

"But . . . they cried out . . . ."

"They were not Romans, Gaius," his teacher said firmly.

"They weren't?" Gaius asked.

"No, they were not Romans," he calmly repeated. "Now lay down, young man, and go to sleep. Such things will never happen to you."

Gaius had laid back down on his bed, listening to the sound of his teacher putting some things away. When he heard the pedagogue at the door of his chamber, ready to leave, he suddenly spoke the question that was plaguing him.

"It's all right because they were not Roman?" Gaius asked.

"Yes."

"But are you Roman?"

"No," his pedagogue said simply. "I am not."

Now, as a grown man in his own home, drinking watered wine and thinking of his father, Gaius felt the same conflict of feeling that had boiled inside him so many years ago. In his professional life, he kept coming into contact with a Judean tax collector, a member of the local community that worked for Rome. They were not equals. The little man was not a Roman, after all. He was not a citizen of full rights and respect. He was a Judean, clamoring for a little favor from the Roman Empire. Gaius did not blame Zacchaeus. He did not blame him for seeing the glory of Rome and longing to touch the fringe of her robes. In fact, he liked Zacchaeus a great deal. And he pitied him. He pitied his solitude, his loneliness.

It was that solitude that was frightening. To see a man separated from his society, cut off from the friendships and relationships that should sustain him was terrible. It was uncomfortable. He felt the poor little man reaching out to him, trying to establish a friendship that could not be. Gaius was a Roman, a centurion. He associated with Zacchaeus for professional reasons only. He could not fill that gaping hole. He did not want to. Yet despite this, he could not stop thinking about the man.

He found himself asking the same question he had asked as a small boy, but now he had more words . . .

The pain was all right because he wasn't Roman. Wasn't it?

CHAPTER 13

The Moneylender

Seth paused midstride in the street and raised his hands up to the heavens. He closed his eyes and raised his voice to be clearly heard.

"I thank You, Adonai, God of the Universe, for the gift of one more day to serve Your mighty Name!"

He stayed in that position, his hands raised, feeling the foot traffic of the street milling past him. He knew that people were looking at him. He knew that they were thinking how righteous he must be to be overcome with thanksgiving while walking in the street. He knew that word would pass about Seth, the moneylender, who worshipped even as he walked.

Seth lowered his hands, opened his eyes and looked mildly around himself at the staring townspeople who quickly averted their glances once they were noticed. He gave a small, serene smile and resumed his contented amble down one of the streets of Yericho.

Yes, he was truly thankful that Elohim had created him to be who he was. He was thankful, firstly, that he was not a woman. To be a woman would be unforgiveable. They were weak, easily confused, and sinful to the core. He was also thankful that Elohim had blessed him with the Pharisee pedigree that made him one of Adonai's chosen. He was thankful that Elohim had given him the family he did, with the wealth that clearly showed His favor. He was thankful that God had blessed him with intelligence and an affinity for numbers. Seth knew himself to be a righteous man, helping his fellow Jews by lending them his own personal money . . . putting coins in their hands when they had none of their own to rub together . . . for a small fee.

Seth noticed a familiar woman walking in front of him and he let out a low hum of admiration. He watched the sway of her hips and smiled to himself. A woman might be sinful to the core, she might even make him long to sin, but there was nothing evil in a

thought that he would not act on. She was of average height . . .
shorter than he was. She had a good build, solid and curving. He
liked the way she moved.

Seth picked up his pace and then made a show of looking to the
side as if searching for a particular building. As he turned, he felt her
soft body collide with his and stiffen with alarm as his arm pulled
around her.

"Pardon me, madam," he said, sincerity booming through his
voice. He released her, but not before he made a show of making
sure she stayed on her feet, keeping her close against him a few moments longer than absolutely necessary.

"I'm sorry, sir, I do apologize," she murmured, but something
more defiant flashed in her eyes as her steely gaze met his.

"Tzofit?" he said. "Wife of my dear friend, Oshri?"

"Yes," she said, suddenly flustered. "Yes, but—"

"I'm sorry for your loss, dear woman," he said. "Your husband
was a good man."

"Thank you," she said, her attention moving past Seth once
more. She was on her way somewhere, but he was not yet finished
with her.

"Life must be lonely for you," Seth said. "Lonely and uncertain."

"Elohim will provide, sir," she said, her tone tense. She looked
at him, something hard and sharp flickering underneath the fragile
surface of her demeanor.

"Yes, yes . . ." he sighed. "Elohim will provide . . . but sometimes life is more difficult than we deserve, is it not?"

He was alluding to Oshri's undeserved difficulties and she did
not answer, but brushed past him, leaving him chuckling in amuse-
ment. Yes, he'd heard many stories of Tzofit. Oshri had confided at
great length about his difficult marriage.

"You have never heard a voice more dripping with disdain,"
Oshri had said, shaking his head. "If you slap her, she stares at you,
mutely. If you shout at her, she is unshaken. She is like a stone."

"You shout at her?" Seth had asked.

"Not I," Oshri had shaken his head. "But my mother has re-
peatedly. And I would have slapped my wife if my mother had not."

"She seems to be . . ." Seth cleared his throat. ". . . moderately
well behaved in public."

"Stop to talk with her, and if you do not see the signs, I will call myself a camel!" Oshri had declared. "Difficult, waspish, angry, rude. She can set a plate before you, eyes downcast, and still make you worried to take the first bite."

Yes, a woman like Tzofit made Seth glad that Elohim had not created him a woman. A woman was born to bring comfort for men, and this woman had failed her duties.

Seth was a man who understood how a woman like Tzofit could rule a poor man so absolutely. While he longed to take another wife or a mistress to be a comfort to him, Oshri would never do so. A woman of perfection like Rachel from the stories of old could be enjoyed alongside her sister, Leah, and two concubines. While a good woman was as easy to tame as a small bird, and as happy with more birds about her as ever could be, Tzofit was a different animal all together. She was a shrew.

Strange that while Seth loathed Tzofit and despised all the characteristics that she wore like bangles about her wrists, he did not want to take his eyes off of her swaying hips.

"Oh, Elohim, King of the Universe," Seth whispered, his eyes clinging to her retreating form. "I thank You that You did not create me a woman!"

And for this he was truly thankful, because as a woman, he would not be able to appreciate the appeal of a truly sinful female.

Dassah shook the flour off her hands and planted them firmly on her hips. She stood in the courtyard, looking toward the door that led into the family home. She was motionless, her eyes fixed on nothing in particular.

"Mother?"

Dassah turned and gave her daughter, Nitza, a questioning look.

"Are you worried?" Nitza asked.

"Bah," was all Dassah said, giving a wave of her hand and turning back to the dough she had been kneading. "Worry can't move a stone."

It was one of Dassah's mother's sayings, and it brought her comfort to use it. However, Dassah was worrying. She would not tell her 12-year-old daughter this, though. No, worry was not to be shouldered by children, even if the child was old enough to become a wife in her own right. Worry was for Dassah to carry on her own shoulders. Her worries were not the worries of an average wife, concerned over marriage arrangements for her children, worry over a sick loved one. She was worried about something different. She was worried that she was going crazy.

The thought had always been one that nagged the back of her mind. And she had reason. Dassah's sister, Ophrah had seemed like a normal girl. She had laughed and played, giggled, and told secrets. She had been a normal girl, just like Dassah had been. Ophrah was one year older, and of all of Dassah's siblings, they had been the closest in age. When Ophrah turned 13 and their parents announced that they had a husband arranged for her, everything seemed to change.

At first, Ophrah was nervous, as all girls were when they discovered they were about to become wives. But it went further than that. Ophrah begged her parents not to marry her to that man. She claimed that his family followed her about. She claimed that they watched her while she slept. While Dassah had struggled to understand what her sister was saying, her parents had exchanged a significant look. Dassah had crept out of her bed that night and listened at the door to her parents' bedroom where they were talking.

". . . like Aunt Rivka . . ."

"Your aunt got the condition, didn't she?" her mother was asking. "She had it!"

"Not until she lost her first baby," her father said, his voice low. "But then she got it . . ."

"What did she do?" her mother asked, her voice low. "I mean, how did you know she had it?"

"I didn't see much as a boy, but I heard my father discussing it with his brothers, not knowing how to deal with her," her father had said. "She used to think that the tanner was following her. She had to be forced to eat. She said that the tanner was trying to poison her food. She always heard a baby crying and kept going out to find it so she could soothe it."

There was a pained silence.

"And Ophrah?" her mother asked.

There was more silence.

"We must never speak of it," her father finally said. "We will be shamed to have more insanity in the family. We will be shamed." His voice broke.

That was when Dassah crept back to her sleeping mat, her heart heavy. Ophrah had the condition. She'd heard it whispered about. It was the craziness that afflicted some families. When somebody had it, there was no getting better. One day they disappeared and no one spoke of them again.

Now, as a grown woman with grown children, Dassah was thinking of her sister. One day, Ophrah had disappeared, and no one ever spoke of her again. But that didn't take away the affliction . . . the craziness that bled its way through the family. That didn't take away the possibility that Dassah would one day find herself afflicted, too.

"Mother, you *are* worrying!" Nitza said. "Is there something wrong? Is someone sick?"

"No, dearest," Dassah said, giving her youngest daughter a reassuring smile. "No one is sick."

But she wasn't so sure.

Ehud was a good, honest man. He was a kind and considerate husband. He always provided well. Yet she could not shake the feeling that something was horribly wrong. This, in itself, did not make Dassah crazy. No, a woman felt things that she could not explain all the time. What confused her was the fact that she had seen her husband in strange places. She saw him creeping along the wall, looking over it at their neighbors. She saw him standing in the marketplace, but when she turned to gather her purchase and go to greet him, he would be gone. She had seen him crouched by an open window in the twilight.

Like any other woman, Dassah had at first assumed that her husband was hiding something from her. Perhaps a mistress. But it didn't add up. Nothing added up. Nothing made sense. When she talked to him about it, gently asking him if she had seen him in various places, he had looked at her, shaken his head, and asked if she *thought* she'd seen him. It was a question that Dassah preferred not to answer.

Ordinarily, Dassah would not have been worried about herself. But considering her sister's weakness in the head, Dassah was always a little bit afraid. What if she was the confused one? What if the things she thought she saw were not real at all? What if she had the condition?

A larger part of Dassah, however, was pragmatic. If she was not crazy, then her husband was hiding something. What Ehud could possibly be hiding, she did not know. A mistress was her biggest fear, but even that she could survive. She had her daughter, her youngest, beautiful girl. As long as she had her children, her husband could not truly break her heart.

But deep inside Dassah's belly she felt it. Something, whether it was in her own head or her husband's, something was not right.

ᴄHE MᴀᴄᴄH

Zacchaeus knew that when his father summoned him again, the news could not be good. His mind went back to the first time he remembered being summoned by his father. He couldn't have been more than 5 years old. He had tried to steal a grapevine from a neighbor by digging it up and "transplanting" it next to their house. The hacked apart vine and trail of soil told the story.

"Zacchaeus," his father had said, his voice deadly quiet. "Do you know why I've called you?"

Zacchaeus, still naïve enough to believe that his father knew nothing about the vine, cheerfully shook his head in the negative. He paid for that cheer with a few smart strokes with a twig on his backside.

The next time Zacchaeus remembered being summoned, he was close to 8 years old. He had hidden behind a thicket of bushes, waiting for the girls to come with their water jars. He had listened to their conversation as they paused to chat, and the next day, when he walked past them on their errand for water, he'd begun to sing a song he'd made up about the things he'd overheard. It had beautiful rhythm and clever rhyme, and apparently it was so memorable that it was repeated word for word to his parents.

"Zacchaeus," his father had said in that now familiar tone. "Do you know why I've called you?"

Zacchaeus had experienced a rush of pride when his father repeated the song back to him, word for word, but he'd paid for his cleverness with a few more strokes of a leather thong across his backside.

The next time Zaccchaeus remembered being summoned by his father, he was nearly 14. He had been talking with a group of boys, and they had been making fun of him as they always did. Zacchaeus had had enough, so he decided to get even. He told them that he had dreamed the night before that Rabbi Malachi's serving girl was sneaking away to visit one of the merchants by the well. It was a place known to be deserted at high noon because of the heat. The boys had laughed, and Zacchaeus had earnestly insisted that he believed himself to be a prophet. Finally, after much disbelief, Zacchaeus asked them to place a bet with him to see if his "dream" had been true. They complied, and when Zacchaeus led them to the well, they had burst upon the rabbi's serving girl and a young merchant, whom, truth be told, Zacchaeus had been spying on for some time.

"Zacchaeus, do you know why I've called you?" his father had asked.

And this time, Zacchaeus knew exactly why his father had called him.

"It is blasphemous to claim to be a prophet!" his father had roared. "Not only have you blasphemed Elohim, but now a marriage must be arranged for a merchant's son and a serving girl. Never has there been such an unequal marriage in Yericho!"

And Zacchaeus had leaned over and accepted the stinging lashes to his backside, secretly pleased that his father hadn't known about the betting, and that he would be able to keep the loot he'd finagled out of the other boys. A whipping was a small price to pay for this victory.

So today, as a grown man, when his father summoned him for a discussion, he felt the same anxiety from boyhood . . . even more so. After their conversation about Tzofit, he feared that this could not be good news. Out of habit, alone, he did a quick mental inventory of any recent sins that his father could have discovered. He came up empty.

"Son," Chayim said, putting a hand firmly on Zacchaeus' shoulder. "Do you know why I've called you?"

This time, however, Zacchaeus thought that he knew exactly why his father had called for him. He had a marriage arranged for him, and Zacchaeus had obligations. It was like walking into a whipping with his eyes wide open, and his father was pushing him steadily forward toward his punishment.

"I have an idea," he said slowly. He gave his father an uneasy smile and poured himself a cup of fresh goat milk, more for distraction than because he wanted to drink it.

"Don't you ever think of when you should claim your wife?" Chayim asked.

"It is not for me to think of," Zacchaeus hedged. "It is for my father to decide."

"And it has already been decided," Chayim said, folding his hands carefully in front of him.

"You have not reconsidered?" Zacchaeus asked, his voice low.

"No."

They were silent. They stood in the courtyard under the gnarled branches of the ancient olive tree. The olives were full size now, but still green, hanging like heavy dew drops off the leafy branches. Zacchaeus sighed heavily and rubbed the heels of his hands over his eyes.

"My complete dislike of Tzofit changes nothing?" he asked.

"Marriage is a complicated state, my son," Chayim said by way of answer. "A woman has a role to fill, as does a man. If both fulfill their duties, then the home may be at peace."

"Are you suggesting that Oshri did not fulfill his duty?"

"*She* is our duty!" Chayim exclaimed, his patience evaporating. "The fact will not go away because we want it to. It will not change. Our duty remains before us, and the clan is watching to see that we take care of it. What would you have me do?"

Zacchaeus shook his head mutely. He knew the situation. He knew that their honor depended upon this union. And he knew that his happiness must be sacrificed for the clan.

"This is not easy for me, son," Chayim said, his tone softening. "I do not like to do this."

"Nor do I," Zacchaeus said woodenly.

"If I could arrange for you differently, I would," his father said.

Zacchaeus nodded.

"However," Chayim went on, "I called you here today to discuss the timing of the wedding."

"What of it?" Zacchaeus asked. "You should know that I care nothing for the details."

"It is time for you to start preparing a wedding chamber for your bride," his father said simply. "The wedding must happen soon."

Zacchaeus laughed bitterly. "A wedding chamber!"

"I have been thinking," Chayim said. "Perhaps the house you already own would be a nice home for yourself and Tzofit . . ."

"My house?" Zacchaeus snapped. "I don't want her in it."

"It would be easier on your mother, I think."

"To have *me* away from her?"

"To have Tzofit in a different house for a while," Chayim said, pursing his lips. "It has been difficult, to say the least, these last few years. I do not anticipate that it will improve. But perhaps, if Tzofit were mistress of her own home, you might be able to . . ." He seemed at a loss for words.

"Take her in hand?" Zacchaeus asked with a bitter laugh.

"It wouldn't have to be permanent, son."

Zacchaeus did not reply, but he looked up as his mother entered the courtyard. Her soft eyes were filled with pity and guilt as she looked across at her son.

"Congratulate me, mother," Zacchaeus said, his voice low and angry. "I am to be married very soon."

"May Adonai bless you, my son," she whispered, her voice barely audible.

"I certainly hope He will!" Zacchaeus retorted, walking briskly away from his parents and toward the door that led into the house. "If anyone deserves a solid blessing, it will be me for enduring the punishment of a pagan!"

Tzofit saw the look of victory on her mother-in-law's face immediately, and it scared her. She was bent over the millstone, grinding grain into flour, her body rocking with the rhythmic motion of the stone going in the slow, grating circles. She did not stop grinding, but her stomach tightened in apprehension.

"Tzofit," Shahar said. "I need to speak with you."

Tzofit stopped grinding and sat back on her heels, wiping her hands on an apron she had tied around her waist for the purpose. Shahar stood, a smile crinkling the corners of her lips, looking down at her daughter-in-law.

"I have news," Shahar said, waiting expectantly for a reply.

"Oh?" Tzofit said.

"You are to be married very soon. I congratulate you," Shahar said.

Tzofit nodded, willing her expression to be blank. She loathed giving her mother-in-law any glimpse of her emotions, wishing she could hide behind a veil.

"May I ask to whom?" she asked carefully.

"To your husband's brother," Shahar said, the first sign of insecurity breaking through her polished happiness.

"Zacchaeus," Tzofit said, her stomach sinking. She was to be married to a dwarfed tax collector. If the insult were not complete, this was the very man she had grown to loathe over the years of her marriage. For the first time in a long, long time, she had the urge to break down and cry.

"Do you have a problem with this arrangement?" Shahar asked, her spine suddenly stiff and her head cocked to an angle that told Tzofit her mother-in-law was getting her hackles up.

"I would not be foolish enough to criticize my new husband to his mother," Tzofit replied thinly.

"Is he not good enough for you?" Shahar snapped. "Is he too short? Is he too worldly for the likes of you?"

"I haven't spoken," Tzofit replied.

"Well, let me tell you, girl!" Shahar was visibly shaking. "You are nothing more than the unfortunate widow of a man who was socially higher than any of your kin. Don't forget it! You married up, Tzofit. We took you because we thought you were beautiful, not because you had any value of your own!"

"Yet here I am," Tzofit said.

"Here you are," Shahar said. "For now."

"For now?" Tzofit mentally chastised herself for vocalizing her thoughts so quickly.

"You will not be living in this house any longer," Shahar said. "When your new husband comes for you, you will be living with him in a separate home."

Her new husband. Tzofit noticed that Shahar refused to use her son's name. Did it sound better to speak of a husband of the generic variety rather than identify the pathetic runt she would be tied to for the rest of her life? Tzofit's shock and dismay was quickly melting into anger. Anger was an emotion she preferred. It was an emotion of strength, not weakness. It was easier to wield than sorrow was. It was easier to carry than regret or despair.

"I will not be living here?" Tzofit said.

"Did you not hear me?" Shahar threw her hands in the air and sighed. "No, you will no longer live here. You will live in a new home."

Tzofit's situation was beginning to dawn on her. She would not be here, with the people she had grown accustomed to. She would no longer live in the only home she'd lived in after leaving her parents. She would be in a house, alone, with Zacchaeus. There would be no other family. No other people to cushion the adjustment. Only herself and the tax collector whom she hated . . . who hated her with equal passion. Alone.

"Mother!" Tzofit said suddenly, respect entering her tone. "Please, don't throw me from this house. Let me stay with you."

"Now I am 'Mother'?" Shahar asked with a small laugh. "I can understand your fear, young woman. I can understand it."

Tzofit was silent. She clamped her lips together and watched the older woman's eyes, looking for some softness.

"I would be afraid, too," Shahar said after a moment. "Going from a home where I could act as snippy and ungrateful as I liked to a home where not one misstep would be accepted. Yes, I would be afraid."

Tzofit felt the anger coming back up, and she struggled to hide the disgust that she knew would register through her eyes.

"I would pack, if I were you," Shahar said. "Your husband will come for you in the very near future, and what you have not packed, will remain here indefinitely."

Tzofit pushed herself to her feet, stretching the ache out of her legs. She focused her attention on very carefully brushing the dust from the palms of her hands.

"Tzofit?" Shahar said.

"Yes?" she replied.

"I congratulate you," Shahar said, a smile spreading across her face. "You have rid yourself of a mother-in-law, but you have certainly gained a master."

CHAPTER 15

BURDENS

Ehud had always been a good man. He had always prayed at appropriate times, kept the Sabbath laws and kept his women in check. He had always been a good man, but today as he walked home, returning to the weaving business where he'd work by lamplight late into the evening to fill the extra orders he had taken above the day's workload, he was worried. He knew that obeying Elohim's laws made him righteous, but he felt that something was missing. None of his blessings prayed over food, none of his murmured prayers as he touched doorposts, none of his intoned blessings over his home and family brought him comfort.

As he approached the door to his home, he reached out and touched the doorpost, murmuring the familiar words.

"Hear O Israel, Adonai is Elohim and Adonai is One."

His only comfort was that his wife did not know what he had done. She did not know that their lives were suspended by a spider's thread. She could still sweetly enjoy her home free of this crushing worry. He felt that he had done well in this. He was a good provider, and he was a good protector. She was but a simple woman, and giving her such a burden was cruelty. She could not understand the workings of the male financial world. She was a woman, after all. He smiled tenderly, thinking of his wife's trusting gaze. Yes, she was woman.

"You lying, scheming snake!"

The words hit him like a rock to the head and he stared in shocked amazement at the woman before him. His wife stood, her hair uncovered and disheveled, her hands planted on her hips. She was quivering with fury, her eyes snapping fire, her lips parted, and her fingers clenched. She was a daunting sight, yet he had a sudden realization that she was beautiful. He'd never seen her this way before . . . never in the 20 years of their marriage had he seen her in such a state, and a small part of his mind regretted it.

"What is that stupid smile on your face?" she snapped. "If you knew what has happened in this home, husband, you would not be so pleased with yourself!"

The surprised smile faded from his lips, replaced by his own rage. How dare she speak to him this way? He was her master and lord! He was man of this house, and her place was to respect him.

"You—" Her finger shook as she pointed it at him, looking down the length of it and into his face. "You! You made me think I was crazy!"

"Dassah—" He didn't have the words to answer her.

"Like my sister, you said! Confused! Simple!" She spat the words out with venom.

"Dassah, this is disobedient!" he barked. "Stop it, now!"

"Then I will be disobedient," she retorted. "And what will you do now? You've already ruined us!"

Ehud stiffened.

"Yes, I know all about it, husband," she said. "Look at her! Look!"

He followed his wife's shaking finger to where his youngest daughter sat, her face tearstained and ashen. She sat with her back against the wall and her knees pulled up to her chest with a white knuckled grip.

"What has happened to you, Nitza?" he demanded, fear rising up in his chest like water. "Nitza, what is this?"

She was silent, and tears welled up in her eyes and spilled down her cheeks. She looked at him with that same look she used to give him when she was a little baby and he didn't know what she wanted or how to help her. Now, at 12 years old she was nearly a woman, and she still looked at him with the same expression that had melted his heart for all these years. But he was frightened this time. Truly, deeply frightened.

"Has a man touched you?" he blurted out. It was his worst fear that a man should take advantage of his precious daughter. "Who was it? Who dared to lay a finger on you?"

Nitza was still silent, so Ehud turned his rage onto his wife, grabbing her roughly by the arm and shaking her.

"Tell me, woman!" he roared.

"No man has touched her," Dassah said coolly. "Yet."

"What do you mean?" he shouted. "You had better spit it out all at once, Dassah, or so help me!"

He let the threat hang in the air, knowing that she knew better than to fear him. She snatched her arm out of his grip and moved toward their daughter, crouching down next to her and stroking the girl's tangled hair.

"We had a visit from a friend of yours," Dassah said, her voice low and crooning as if trying to soothe a baby. "He said that you owe more money than we could ever repay. He said that if you do not give him the full amount in two days time . . ."

Her voice cracked, and Ehud saw for the first time the desperation and terror behind her anger. She paused and took a wavering breath.

"What?" Ehud whispered. "What would he do?"

"He would take Nitza as a slave."

The room was silent except for his daughter's stifled sobs. Ehud felt himself start to shake and he sank to his knees. He did not feel the jarring crack as his knees hit the packed dirt floor. All he felt was the suffocation of his chest filling up with unshed tears.

"Oh, Nitza," he whispered.

"Abba," she said, her voice plaintive. "You can pay him, can't you?"

Ehud was silent.

"Husband," Dassah said, her voice low and angry. "Do something."

"Do what?" he asked, shaking his head. "Do what?"

"If that beast takes my girl," Dassah said, the threat dripping from her voice. "If that beast takes my little girl from me . . . so help *me*, husband. So help *me*!"

Nitza looked out the window into the night sky, her hands shaking. She clasped them together to still them, but the fear still throbbed through her body. Debt. Money. Anger. Being taken away. Being all alone. The thoughts were jumbled up inside of her and she did not know what to do. Would her father repay the money? He had to. If not, that evil man would take her away from her parents. She may never see them again! The thought was crushing and terrifying and made the tears start falling all over again.

Abba loved her. He wouldn't let this happen. Abba always took care of things. But he had looked so . . . afraid. His fear had terrified her. She'd been waiting for him to reassure her, to say that she need not worry because he would fix everything. She'd been waiting all day to hear those words. And then all evening. And now she stood looking out the window, still waiting to hear those words from someone. Anyone.

"Oh, Elohim," she whispered. "I am only a girl. I am not even a woman. I don't want to be a slave. I don't want to leave my parents. Help me, Adonai!"

"Nitza?"

She turned to see her father standing behind her in a pool of moonlight. His eyes were puffy and red, and his face looked suddenly worn and very old. His hands hung limply at his sides.

"Abba?" she said.

"I'm so sorry, little girl," he said, tears catching his voice. "I'm so sorry!"

"But you will fix it, won't you?" she asked. "You can pay it back?"

"I will try my best," he said quietly. "But if I fail . . ."

"No, you won't!" she cried. "You can't fail!"

"If I do fail, little girl," he said, his voice trembling. "There are some things you must know."

She was silent, looking up into her abba's face.

"If that man takes you away, you must remember that I will come for you," he said. "I will do anything . . . anything at all to get you back. Do you understand?"

"But I don't want to leave you," she whispered in terror. "Please, Abba, don't let him take me."

Her father stepped forward and wrapped his arms tightly around her, so tight that she could barely breathe. She listened to the hammering of his heart in his chest and she heard the rattle of his breathing.

"Nitza," he whispered. "Even if I fail, I will come for you."

And that was the moment Nitza realized that her father had no way to fix this.

Benyamin had several things running through his mind while he bowed over the food in front of him. The first was that the food smelled wonderful and it was making his stomach rumble. He also thought that by thinking of the food while he was bowing in prayer, he was sinning. This gave him a pang of guilt and a resolution to lengthen his prayer to make up for his weakness. He wryly realized that his sister was watching him, and that the longer he bowed in prayer, the more righteous she would believe him to be. The resulting pride that surged through him made him feel more guilt. He struggled to focus on the words of his prayer, concluded it, and raised his head.

Bracha stood motionless where she had been when he'd bowed his head, and he felt her eyes on him. He did not look up. Instead he reached for the food, priding himself on his smooth, decorous movements while he slurped the lentils into his mouth with a mouthful of flatbread.

"Brother," Bracha said softly.

He grunted, showing he'd heard her, but still did not look up.

"Benyamin," she said, coming closer so that her bare feet were in his line of vision. They were washed, as a woman's feet should be, and rough with calluses from her long, daily walks. He chewed hungrily, gulping back the food as he absently looked at her feet.

"Milk," he said, holding up an empty cup, and she quickly ran to bring the pitcher of frothing goat's milk. He drained the cup, the sweet creamy milk coating his mouth and giving him the enjoyable grassy aftertaste he had loved since boyhood.

"Benyamin," she repeated, sinking down to his side.

He looked up at her, reaching for more lentils as he did so. His hunger being filled, he felt his irritation draining away and he gave her a smile.

"Why do you look so worried, Bracha?" he asked.

"I worry about you," she said.

"Me?" He let out a low laugh, plunging his bread into the pot of stewed lentils and expertly curving it in his fingers to bring it up to his mouth brimming with food.

"Benyamin," she said earnestly. "I don't know what you are planning, brother. I am a woman, and I would never be so disrespectful as to ask into your plans, but I worry all the same."

"Of what?"

"Of . . . of . . ." she stopped, shaking her head. "I don't know. Perhaps I am only being weak, Ben, but you seem different in the last few weeks. You seem changed."

"Perhaps I am," he said. And he meant it. He felt the change, too. There was something about responsibility that squared a man's shoulders. There was something about the responsibility one took in a task for Adonai Almighty that showed a man his importance in the eyes of his Creator, even if not in the eyes of the world. He might be only a poor laborer, but he was someone. The burden might be heavy, but he was worthy of carrying it.

"Are you all right?" she asked quietly.

"I am fine, Bracha," he said, giving her a reassuring smile. "It is very sweet of you to worry about your brother, but I am fine."

She was silent, obviously brooding. There was something she was getting at, but was afraid to say it. As she should be. Women did not meddle in men's actions. They let them be. They fed the men. They cared for them. And they kept their noses out of their business. It was the righteous way.

But there was something so sweet and melancholy about his sister squatting there, her big eyes brimming with emotion and her lips pressed together. It reminded him of their childhood years spent playing together, and something inside of him softened.

"Just say it," he said with a shrug, and she looked at him in surprise.

"Pardon?" she said.

"Just say it, Bracha," he said. "You are my sister, and if you sit there with that look on your face, you will ruin my digestion. Just say it."

"I don't want to anger you," she said uncertainly.

He gave a dismissive wave of his hand and rolled his eyes at her. Her worried expression broke into a rueful smile.

"I'm worried because I sense that you are about to do something," she said. "I don't know what, and I can't ask what. But I sense that it is something that will change you forever."

"Everything changes us," he said. "Everything scratches us somehow."

"True," she said. "But some things scratch and some things cut. You have been growing angrier. You have been walking like a man under a heavy load. I know that the man's world is not understood by women, and I know that your burdens are your own . . ."

Her words trailed away, and Benyamin looked at her, wondering whether she deserved his anger or not. He didn't feel anger, but he did not need to feel anger to give her a much needed tongue-lashing. He could be as calm and collected as a glass of water and still do his duty as her male relative. However, he was caught between putting her in her place and hearing her out. She looked down at her feet, her hands clasped firmly together in front of her.

"It is true. You know nothing about a man's world," he said shortly.

"But I know about you, dear Ben," she said, raising her eyes to meet his. "I know about you."

Her soft eyes were disarming and he felt himself wishing he could confide in her like he used to when they were so much younger. But he was a man now, and men did not show that kind of weakness. He knew his responsibility. He knew what he had to do for Elohim, for Judah, for all Jews. He knew what he must do to make Rome bleed.

Killing the tax collector would not be easy. It would not be clean. It would not be pleasant. But it would be right.

That was not a burden that a woman could help him carry.

CHAPTER 16

Zacchaeus Plans a Party

Zacchaeus slammed his cup onto a table with more force than necessary. It was also more force than the clay cup could withstand, and a crack snaked its way down the side. He picked up a handful of nuts then tossed them back into the bowl in irritation.

He was about to be married. After years of dreaming of the pleasure of having a wife of his own . . . a wife to cook for him and to make his home happy with the sound of her soft voice . . . After years of longing, his wish was about to come true. But like all things in his life, it was twisted, and the woman who was about to be bound to him for life was none other than Tzofit.

Tzofit! He truly loathed her. He could not pretend to feel anything but dislike for the sour woman. Yet she was the one to share his bed. She was the one to bear him children . . . to bear his dead brother's children, in reality. The babies to be born would not be attributed to his name at all. Even the pleasure of children to take his name was being denied him, it seemed.

How would it be, living in the same house with Tzofit? The thought frightened him a little. She wasn't one to obey a husband. Nor was she one to meekly accept her situation. Would she do as he ordered her to do? Would she respect his authority? Would she humiliate him in public? Would she defy him in private? Could he bring himself to sire an heir through her?

"Master?"

Calev, Zacchaeus' chief servant, stood respectfully to the side, his eyes cast downward. Zacchaeus realized that he'd been standing motionless beside the table for some time and he gave himself a mental shake.

"I need nothing," Zacchaeus snapped.

"I simply want to prepare for future . . . needs," the man said deftly, the pause barely perceptible.

"Yes, I will soon be married," Zacchaeus said. "If that is what you are asking."

"Yes, sir," Calev said. "Shall I prepare quarters for the honored lady?"

"She is hardly a lady," Zacchaeus retorted, but he felt a laugh rising up at his little joke. The servant's lips twitched upward at the humor.

"Yes, you should prepare a room for her," Zacchaeus sighed. "She will not be lodging with me."

"Perhaps the room next to yours?" he asked carefully.

"No, no," Zacchaeus chuckled. "As far from mine as you can arrange."

The chief servant nodded and looked expectantly at Zacchaeus, waiting to be dismissed, his expression a mixture of deference and entitlement.

"This is difficult to celebrate," Zacchaeus said thoughtfully. "Very difficult, indeed."

"I agree," the man said, his voice low. "But what a party, if you don't mind me saying, sir."

Zacchaeus was silent, looking at his chief servant with newfound respect. It was difficult to remember that this man who served him daily was not simply a tool, but was also a man. No, marrying Tzofit was not something to celebrate, but it did pose a certain opportunity that he could not deny. A wedding was a social event that the community participated in. It was a social necessity.

"What a party!" Zacchaeus said thoughtfully, for the first time his heart beginning to lighten.

"You are a man with impeccable taste, sir," Calev said quietly.

Taste. Yes, Zacchaeus was a man with taste. He liked expensive things. He liked to display his wealth in artful ways. He enjoyed shopping for the right fabrics, the right couches, the right tapestries woven in Asia Minor. He enjoyed the feel of Chinese silks and delicate Indian cottons. He was sensitive to the mingling elements of fine Arabian myrrh, of the sensuous undertones of nard. He appreciated fine wine vintages and was willing to buy olive oil from the caravans that originated as far away as North Africa in order to enjoy the delicate flavor the local oil makers were not able to achieve. Zacchaeus was certainly a man with taste, but there were few who appreciated it. In order to recognize his exceptional preferences, one would have to visit Zacchaeus in his home.

He had been preparing for this day for as long as he could re-member. Zacchaeus had played the dinner over and over again in his mind. He had perfected the menu. He had tweaked his mental preparations until the décor was absolutely perfect. From the light-ing and the artful seating to the entertainment and Zacchaeus' own welcoming speech, a party of this magnitude was exactly what Zacchaeus had dreamed of since he was a young man.

"Calev!" Zacchaeus said suddenly. "Fetch a tablet. We are about to make a guest list."

At a party . . . at the perfect party, the guest list must be as artis-tically exquisite as the very tapestries that hung on the walls. It must be as balanced as the wine's fragrant flavors. It must be as compli-mentary and intentional as the expertly prepared dinner courses, as subtle and warm as the evening lamplight.

A party began and ended with the guest list.

Gaius Markus Africanus had debriefed the centurion replacing him and executed a precise and efficient shift change. There was something satisfying in Roman precision. While the soldier in him knew that well-practiced and well-executed commands were like overlapping armor, there was another part of him that enjoyed the seamless transitions for whole different reasons. He liked the feeling of power it gave him to have a single uttered command create the symmetrical fanning of armored soldiers and the beautiful clash of fists against armored chests. One word and 70 men stepped out with perfect, precise unity. It was a thing of beauty.

Age seemed to change the way Gaius saw things. Fifteen years ago, he would have seen power and possibility in the gleam of that armor, but now. . . now, that his hair was turning gray and he had nearly 25 years of service under him, he saw details he had missed in the arro-gance of youth. He saw the youthful vitality in those young faces. He saw the agile limbs and the cocky assurance in their steel eyes. And somehow, he always saw another image of each face—the way he knew the man would look if he was dead. It was part of the job. It was part of life. A dead body had meant little to him in years past, but now that he was closer to the end of his life than he was to the beginning of it, dead youths left a bitter taste in his mouth . . . a bitter taste that could only be washed out with several hours of drinking.

As a young man, Gaius had very little fear of death. He would face it gladly, baring his teeth in the face of his own mortality. He'd been foolhardy, the way most young soldiers were. He'd believed in Rome. He'd believed that if he lost his life, it would count for something. Yet now, with his temples turning gray and lines forming around his eyes, Gaius feared death very much. He had a great deal to lose and he had a lingering doubt that when his turn came to dip his foot into the River, that his crossing would contribute to anything substantial at all. His military position would be filled by a younger man, eager to prove himself. His son would accept the inheritance his father left behind. The hole he left behind would almost immediately be swallowed up. Yes, Gaius had a great deal to lose.

It was then, when Gaius was thinking these dismal thoughts, that he saw her. At first he didn't recognize her with her head covered and her quick, furtive steps, but then a splash of light from a torch illumined her face and he recognized her immediately. She was the Jewish girl, that beautiful girl that he just couldn't seem to stop thinking about, and without another thought he angled his steps in her direction.

He didn't mean to speak to her. He knew better than that. She would only run away, and a look of terror on that pretty face would do nothing for him. He didn't want to frighten her or dominate her. In fact, he was not exactly sure what he did want. But he knew the sorts of men who occupied the streets of Yericho at this hour and he cringed to think of what they might have in mind.

So he slipped silently through the dim streets of Yericho, keeping that ruffling robe of the Jewish girl in sight. While he did not know what he intended, he did know that the first dog to try and touch her would be facing the point of Roman steel. Of that much, Gaius was certain.

Bracha was not half the fool that she appeared to be, but sometimes the appearance of an empty head served a woman well. Gentle smiles, self-deprecating gestures, and insisting that she did not understand the things that were as plain as her own hand in front of her face had become second nature to her. She knew how to hide her intelligence, and she did so without thinking. A mild woman was not a threat. A woman who understood nothing but the art of cooking and meekly serving seldom inspired a man's rage. A wise woman always had a few tricks up her sleeve to avoid a man's anger.

As she hurried through the streets of Yericho, her thoughts were on her brother. While she meekly claimed to understand nothing of the outside world, and while Benyamin innocently believed her, she had not been all together truthful, may Elohim have mercy. No, she had not been all together truthful. In fact, you might say that she had lied. A girl could not spend her days selling bread in the market, fending off unwanted attention, listening to the gossip of the other vendors, and observing the living, swelling flow of human bodies that pressed past and around her day after long day without learning something about the world outside her home. And while Bracha hid it well, she had a sharp mind that questioned everything. When something didn't make sense, she chewed it over like a dog with a bone until it came together into something logical. Her brother's behavior hadn't made sense, and it had only taken a few times of "overheard" conversation before the details settled into a picture for her. While she knew her brother saw honor and bravery, all she could see was its inevitable conclusion.

The street was dark, and her sandals slapped softly against the uneven cobblestones. Doors were bolted shut, windows were shuttered. The city was sleeping. Or rather the civilized portion of the city slept. Not far away she could hear the sound of male laughter. Behind a door rumbled muffled shouting and then a crash. She heard a sharp slap and a woman's cry. A dog's low growl penetrated the night and she shivered as she saw movement in some shadows. Whether it was the dog or someone watching her, she was not sure, but either one was enough to make her heart pound in terror.

"Elohim protect me," she whispered. "Guard my path."

Bracha knew the dangers of Yericho's streets at night, but her errand could not wait until morning. Her brother's life could very well depend on it. She had no wish to see her brother stripped naked, beaten, then pinned to a stake with iron nails through his ankles and wrists. Crucifixion was Rome's favorite punishment, and the death was horrific. The very thought made her shudder. Not her brother! Not her Benyamin, if she could help it! The murder of a tax collector would not go unnoticed by Rome, regardless of her brother's hopes or passionate beliefs.

She was not far now. Rabbi Malachi's house was only a few

minutes away, but the distance seemed interminable. She took a deep breath, willing her nerves to calm. If anyone could convince her brother to reconsider his horrible course, it was the rabbi from their youth . . . the rabbi who had taught Benyamin who had seemed so promising until Rabbi Malachi sent him home, never to return. Benyamin had not forgiven Rabbi Malachi for his dismissal from the school, but Benyamin still respected him a great deal. Bracha could think of no one better, no one stronger, to talk to her brother.

"Almost there," Bracha whispered to herself. "Almost—"

She heard the swish of blade before she saw anything. She felt the point press into the side of her neck and a rough hand clamp around her arm, jerking her toward a dark alley. It all happened so quickly that she didn't have time to scream before her throat closed shut in fright.

"Good evening, my pretty," a husky voice hissed into her ear. "If you are an obedient girl, this won't hurt a bit."

Bracha was not half the fool she appeared to be, and as she stared into the leering, grime-streaked face of the man who held her, she knew exactly what he wanted.

CHAPTER 17

Bracha's Brother

Calev had gone out for the entire afternoon issuing invitations. Zacchaeus had made himself busy with tax collecting, and when he returned home very late that evening, he found his chief servant occupied as usual, ensuring his master's comfort. Calev's round, moon-like face was placid and calm as he went about his duties. While a lesser servant washed Zacchaeus' feet, gently splashing cool water over the dusty feet then drying them thoroughly with a fresh cloth, Zacchaeus watched Calev issuing orders about dinner preparation. Seeming to sense his master's gaze directed at him, Calev slowly turned and gave Zacchaeus a courteous bow.

"Master," Calev said. "I hope you will find things in order."

"Yes, yes, of course," Zacchaeus said, turning his attention away, feeling unaccountably flustered. He wanted to ask about the invitations, but he was embarrassed to bring up the subject. To his irritation, Calev nodded politely and turned back to his evening work that would be longer still because of his master's late return.

The invitations had been issued and the thought had not left him the entire day as he took care of business. He thought about it while he issued taxes to some small farmers. He thought about it while he listened to the complaints of a potter who accused him of taxing too heavily to line his own pockets. He thought about it as he quietly observed a nondescript laborer paying for some rather expensive fabric in the market, mentally calculating where the man had gotten the money and wondering if it were taxable. The day had passed in the way it always did, except with each passing hour, he wondered if a reply had been issued to his home. He wondered how various invited guests had reacted upon hearing the news of his upcoming marriage. He wondered if they would respond immediately and how many replies would be waiting for him when he returned home. He imagined Calev approaching him with respectful dignity, announcing that five, 15, or even 20 guests had responded with an affirmative. However, he had returned home and Calev had not reacted the way Zacchaeus had imagined he would. This irritated him.

"Calev," Zacchaeus said, and his servant immediately turned and looked at him expectantly.

"Yes, sir?" Calev folded his hands in front of him.

"Have there been any replies?" Zacchaeus asked briskly.

"To your invitations, sir?" Calev asked. "No, sir. Not yet."

"Hmm," Zacchaeus said, trying to cover the disappointment he felt. "Tomorrow morning, then, I'm sure."

"Yes, sir," Calev said. "Not many homes can afford such a large staff as you do, sir. If I may say so, sir, I don't believe that sparing a servant for a message would be easy in the evening time."

"I hadn't thought of that," Zacchaeus said gratefully.

"Most people forget the needs of the host, sir," Calev said. "It is rude, of course, but not rare."

"No, not rare," Zacchaeus agreed. "Thank you, Calev. You may go back to your duties."

Calev gave his master what could have been construed as a look of pity, but as quickly as the expression crossed Calev's face it was gone, replaced by the bland, respectful expression of a servant who knew his place.

Yes, that was what had happened. Of course, people never thought of the host's anxieties or anticipation. They simply responded in their own due time. It was what people did. Tomorrow morning, Zacchaeus was sure that he would have many responses. Everyone looked forward to attending a wedding. They loved the food, the dancing, the laughing, and reconnecting. They loved the gossip most of all, and if there was one thing that Zacchaeus could provide, it would be gossip. The party would be one to talk about for months afterward, and much as he resented it—two people who deeply loathed each other being joined in marriage—it would be something to see.

"Some wine, sir?"

Zacchaeus took the cup from Calev with a sad smile.

"They hate me," he said in a low voice.

"Certainly not, sir!"

"You know it as well as I do," Zacchaeus replied. "No use pretending otherwise."

Calev was silent, his lips pressed together in a thin line.

"It's lonely, Calev," Zacchaeus said after a moment. "It's very, very lonely."

Zacchaeus turned away. It was not good to show too much emotion around the servants. It eroded respect and caused laziness and thieving.

His life was lonely, though. He knew that he could not expect a sudden influx of friends and close companions. He had lived his entire life without the pleasure of popularity and was not foolish enough to expect it now. The loss of his brother, Oshri, had been a bitter blow. Not only had he lost his brother, but he had lost the only true friend he had.

Oshri. Kind, funny Oshri with his ready sense of humor and infectious laughter. Zacchaeus felt a sudden wave of loneliness for his brother. Oshri was another source of companionship he would never have again. He had only one brother, and that brother was dead.

But a woman . . . a woman would be different. Like any man, he had dreamed of the perfect woman. She would be petite. He could not hope that she would be shorter than he was, but only marginally taller would be quite nice. She would be a wonderful cook. She would be kind and soft. She would let her hand linger on his shoulder when she served him his wine, and sometimes when he looked up he would catch her looking at him with a look of tenderness in her eyes. She would awake before he did and he would be tugged into wakefulness by the scent of breakfast cooking and the sound of her melodious voice as she sang to herself as she worked.

A woman would make the community's coldness bearable. She would make his days endurable as he looked forward to seeing her at evening when he returned. She would make his evenings warm and filled with comfortable silences. She would make his nights companionable, and he dreamed of lying in bed with the scent of his wife's freshly washed hair next to him. A woman could make many things better.

He had prayed for a woman. He had prayed for his family to find him a lovely, doting wife. He had prayed for the impossible. He had believed that somehow Elohim would give him something . . . someone . . . to make up for the misery he had endured.

It had been foolish, really. He did not deserve anything from the Almighty. He was not pious. He was not even loyal to his own people. He had joined with the enemy, the occupiers, the winners. He had done something for himself because Elohim Himself knew that Judah would do nothing for him. And now, after all these years of waiting for his father to provide for him, he was being given a woman. Yes, he was being given a woman, but she was nothing like the woman he had prayed for.

That his bride was to be Tzofit made him feel as though Elohim Himself had joined in with the community in laughing at him. In times like these he used to pray and find comfort, but this time there didn't seem to be a point. It seemed that his fate had been decided. At the very least, Zacchaeus longed to host one magnificent party and let their laughter be tinged with just a tiny bit of envy.

Bracha felt her breath slammed out of her body as she hit the ground. Everything seemed to be moving very slowly—especially her mind. Lying on her back, staring up in horror at the man coming down toward her, she slowly pondered that her father would never believe her. Never, ever believe her.

The man was tall and lanky with large hands and a beak of a nose. His mouth was open in a foul grin, his three remaining teeth jutting out like mile markers along a Roman highway. As he dove down onto her, she struggled to roll over, but found herself tangled in the heavy folds of her own robes. His hand covered her mouth as she opened it to scream.

"None of that, my sweet," he hissed. "Keep it down, would you?"

He was on top of her now, one hand clamped over her mouth, a knee planted in her chest and the other hand fumbling with her robes. She jerked and fought, but suddenly stopped when the blade reappeared and the fierce expression in his eyes told her he meant to use it.

"Pretty hair, lady," he whispered, rubbing his greasy fingers through a handful of her long curls. Her stomach roiled. She needed to throw up and instinctively turned her face away from the sight and stench of him, the violation of his touch. Her hair—her crowning glory that she always kept covered—being touched by this pig was more than she could bear.

He bent down over her face, and his putrid breath filled her nostrils and mouth so that she could taste the foul sourness before he touched her lips. As nausea engulfed her, she felt the vomit rise toward her throat.

Elohim! Adonai!

She did not have words for her prayer, only a desperate, silent stretching toward the only One she knew could help her now. Then as she opened her eyes, searching for one last avenue of escape, she saw the flash of steel. At first she thought it was meant for her, and for a fleeting moment braced herself for death. Then she saw that the blade was pressed firmly against her attacker's throat.

"I wouldn't, if I were you," a gravelly voice said in an almost conversational tone. "I realize it's probably been a long time since you've touched a woman, but this will most definitely be your last if you push me."

The steel blade was a Roman short sword, and as her eyes followed it to the hilt, she saw the hand that gripped it and the muscled arm. He was a centurion by the looks of his armor and the plumes on his helmet. His eyes were not looking at her, but were pinned on the greasy man on top of her.

"No harm," the filthy man muttered. "No harm done . . . just talking, we were . . ."

"We'll keep it that way," the centurion replied evenly. "Now get up."

"I can't," the man said. "Not with the blade there."

"You'd better try," came the hard reply.

He struggled to his feet, wincing as the razor sharp blade pressed into his dirt-encrusted neck and drew a clean, fresh line of blood.

"I'd love to kill you," the centurion said. "But I won't. I'd rather not frighten the lady any further tonight. But you can be assured that I will remember your face and I will look for it. In every crowd, on every street I patrol, I will look for your face."

The man swallowed hard, his face ashen and his Adam's apple bobbing. He nodded vigorously.

"The next time I find you, I will also find an excuse."

The threat was heavy in the air, and when the centurion dropped his sword, the man threw himself backward, scrambled through the dirt, and disappeared into the night leaving only the sound of his running footsteps.

"Are you all right, miss?" the centurion asked, and his eyes softened from the cold steel they had been to something much warmer and almost kind. If he weren't a Roman, Bracha would have felt a flood of relief.

Gaius had seen arrested criminals happier to be in his company than this girl seemed to be as he escorted her back to her home. He felt like a lumbering ox next to her. She was slender and small, her hands clutching at her veil, keeping it close around her face so that only her eyes peered out. He didn't blame her. It probably made her feel safer to be covered, as if she could somehow disappear.

"Did he hurt you, miss?" he asked again for the fourth time.

"No," she said.

Well, this was a first verbal reply. It was a step in the right direction. Every time he had spoken to her before this she had either ignored him or simply shaken her head. His gaze fanned over the road ahead of them and he noticed a posted guard. He saluted them and they saluted back. Two of the soldiers made some rude comments about what Gaius must be doing with the young woman. She stiffened at the words.

"I'm sorry about that," he said awkwardly.

She didn't reply, but she didn't try to run away from him either. She obviously saw some value in having an armed escort through the inky, dirty streets of Yericho in the middle of the night.

"What is your name?" he asked her.

She seemed about ready to answer, then seemed to think better of it.

"My name is Gaius," he said, softening his tone. It only occurred to him now that maybe he was frightening her a little. An armed soldier is dressed the way he does to intimidate other armed men. An unarmed woman might feel less than comfortable.

"I am Bracha," she finally relented. "And I must thank you for saving my life."

"What were you doing out there?" he asked.

There was the silence again. Prostitute? He doubted it. Illicit relationship? Again he doubted it. He had had numerous mistresses, and she didn't fit the bill, no matter how much he'd like her to for his own purposes. However, he didn't have much time to consider her nocturnal business as she pointed out her family home. They were in a poor part of town and the little houses and shacks sat in darkness. A few scattered windows had a tiny glimmer of light from a sputtering lamp, but this was not the kind of neighborhood that could afford to waste oil. Her home, however, was fully lit. This did not bode well for the girl, and he knew it.

The door flew open before he had a chance to knock, and he looked down into the face of a young man with a full beard and narrow shoulders. His eyes flashed fury, and the sight of Gaius in full armor didn't seem to diminish his fervor. The man looked strangely familiar.

"What have you done to her, you pig?" he spat.

Gaius put out a hand, planted it in the middle of the young man's chest and gave him a shove back into the house, pulling the girl behind him. He ducked his head to step inside. An old man and woman sat blinking blearily at him, then the woman stood up and went straight to Bracha making wordless soothing noises in the back of her throat.

"What did he do to you?" the young man demanded, turning his attention to Bracha. "I swear by Elohim, if he touched you—"

"Brother," Bracha said, shaking her head. "You misunderstand."

"At this hour of night?" He almost laughed. "You come home looking ruffled and messy at this hour of night, a Roman pig in tow, and I misunderstand?"

"This . . . Roman . . ." she seemed to stumble over the word, "this Roman saved my life, brother. He chased away an attacker, and because of him I am safe."

The young man looked at his sister for a long moment, then back at Gaius, his eyes still glittering in fury. If he left now, Gaius had no doubt that the girl would be at the receiving end of his anger until it was spent.

"Do you have a problem with me?" Gaius asked in a low tone. "I protect your sister when you do not, and you look at me that way?"

"Son, calm down," the old man cautioned. "It is enough for one night. Calm down."

"She did nothing wrong, and she was not defiled in any way that I know of," Gaius said. "Or does her safety concern you less than my presence does?"

"Benyamin," Bracha said, putting a hand on his arm. "I am safe. I was wrong to go out, but I was seeking Rabbi Malachi. That is all."

It was then that Gaius recognized the young man. He was one of the zealots who muttered and cursed at the Roman guards. He'd seen the man throwing stones at armed soldiers and screaming curses. It made sense, and he almost laughed out loud. He shook his head in disgust and turned toward the door, ducking his head and stepping out into the night. When he looked over his shoulder, he saw Bracha staring after him with an unreadable expression on her face. Her lips were parted and her eyes were moist. She inhaled as if about to speak, then froze, her eyes fixed on him.

Gaius paused, almost turned . . . almost turned and went back to her. But he saw her brother's eyes, and he knew that for anything he did, she would receive the beating. He lowered his gaze and turned away.

Leave it to me to fall in love with the sister of a Jewish zealot! he thought ruefully. Whatever goddess was receiving his wife's spiteful prayers was doing right by her.

CHAPTER 18

THE NEW SLAVE

Seth's wife had been complaining for weeks now that she needed another serving girl. How was she supposed to serve his guests without enough staff? How was she supposed to get his dinner prepared on time if she didn't have a girl to fetch the water while the others were busy with the dinner preparations? How was she supposed to hold her head up in front of her friends when she was forced to live like a pauper?

Day after day, week after week, he heard the same complaints. Sometimes he heard them said directly to him. "Husband, I need another serving girl! How can I keep this home to the level that your position and wealth demand?" Sometimes he heard them muttered as she bustled by, preparing yet another late dinner while his stomach rumbled. "If only I had another pair of hands. No one understands what I go through." Sometimes he overheard it while she chatted with her sisters or her mother. "Another serving girl would make my life so much sweeter. All I need is one. How can I face Shoshanna? How can I live knowing that Eva is laughing behind my back?" Regardless of the form the complaints took, Seth heard them daily until he had had enough.

"Woman, you complain like a she-goat!" he bellowed.

"How so?" she asked sweetly. "What do I complain of? I am a very grateful and dutiful wife." She looked hurt.

"You want another serving girl," he said.

"I have spoken to you of that only once," she retorted, and met his eye, challenging him. But he could not admit that he was listening to the conversations of women, or that her quiet sighs to herself bothered his manly contentment. No, to admit that would be to admit weakness.

"Well, I have decided to give you another serving girl," he muttered, knowing that he had been thoroughly beaten.

"Oh, Seth," she sighed, her eyes melting into deep pools of gratitude. "You are such a kind husband. I only mentioned it once, and you thought about it and in your superior wisdom decided to grant me my wish. I thank Elohim for a husband like you. When will I get her?"

"Soon," he said. He wasn't positive in this moment what he felt, but he felt like a competent, strong and manly husband indeed. He was sure that by evening he would feel used and stupid, but in the moment, looking into those adoring eyes, he couldn't quite piece together why.

But Seth was a man who liked his coin. He did not like to waste it on frivolities. He knew what was necessary in public appearance and he knew what his peers would never notice. A fourth serving girl was one of those things that would be passed over like a sack of barley. While he would give his wife her wish, he knew that he would not pay for it. There was a man by the name of Ehud who owed him a substantial amount of money that he was having a great deal of trouble repaying. It was within Seth's legal rights to demand restitution in the form of servile labor. And Ehud had a daughter who was just the right age. She would do nicely.

So without further ado, Seth had sent his burly and obedient servants to collect on a debt. This was not the kind of collection that he liked to oversee personally. It would be far too emotional, with lots of tears, screaming, and recriminations. While he did not pity men who were too stupid to properly provide for their families, and while he felt entirely justified in collecting on the debt, he preferred not to put himself in the middle of chaos. Instead he waited at home, sipping a cup of water and picking at a plate of olives and goat cheese.

He heard the commotion of their arrival, and he purposefully took several minutes smoothing his robes, picking his teeth, and chewing at a chipped fingernail before going out into the courtyard to have a look at his newest acquisition. Then he strolled slowly into the sunlight, his hands clasped behind his back and his ample belly going before him. He pursed his lips thoughtfully and surveyed the scene.

The girl was not tall, and she was on the thin side. He preferred a fatter serving girl with some pretty dimples, but he would have to forget about that. This girl was thin with large eyes and plump lips. Her nose was prominent, but not in a bad way. Though she stood regally erect, she would not look in his direction at all. She seemed to be a spirited one, something he had not counted on, but that interested him nonetheless.

"So what do we have?" Seth asked, coming forward.

The girl turned toward him, her face a mixture of fear and crushing sadness.

"She'd sell well on the market," his servant advised. "You'd get a pretty penny for her, I'd wager. She's got good teeth, strong limbs."

"Hmm," Seth said, slowly circling the girl to get a better view. "Attractive, too."

He watched her for signs of appreciating a compliment from him and found none. She wasn't going to be the kind of serving girl he liked—the kind that wished to please her master in any way she could.

"Or I could keep her," Seth said, pretending to debate more than he was. "She would do nicely here."

"Yes, sir," his servant agreed. "A high quality worker, I'd wager."

Seth put a finger under her chin and lifted her face. He pulled her eyelids up to see the color of the whites of her eyes, pinched her skin, and pulled down her lower lip to get a better look at her even, straight teeth. He nodded to a large clay jug to the side.

"Lift that," he ordered.

She blinked in confusion.

"Pardon me?" she said.

"That jug," he said, slowing his words down as if talking to a simpleton. "Go and lift it up onto your shoulders. I want to see your strength."

Her jaw clenched and she flushed in repressed rage, making him smile to himself. A feisty one! She would be entertaining. She turned stiffly and walked toward the jug. She lifted it with a little struggle, but balanced it nicely on her shoulder.

"Her strength will build," Seth said. He gave an exaggerated shrug. "I'll keep her for now. Sleep her in the storage closet."

"But sir," his servant interjected quietly. "There is room in the servants' quarters for one more."

"I said the storage closet," he replied.

The servant swallowed a reply that seemed ready on his lips, nodded in acceptance of his orders, and turned toward the girl.

"You," he said. "Come with me and I will find you something suitable to wear. You'll be in the kitchens today. We'll start you with fetching water."

As Seth watched his newest acquisition walk away, he gave a soft chuckle. Yes, she would do very nicely indeed.

Nitza glanced up at the servant who was escorting her into the large house. He was an older man with a confident walk. His eyes were kind, however, and she felt slightly comforted at the sight of the crinkles and creases on his face that told of many years of smiles. It all felt like a dream, still. A horrible, terrible nightmare. She wouldn't have been surprised to wake up and find herself in her bed at home, except that the experience kept going and going and going. This dream would not end, no matter how much she longed for it to evaporate.

"What is your name?" the man asked.

"Nitza."

"Well, Nitza, life is going to be very different for you," he said matter-of-factly. "You are now a slave. Your master owns you, and that is very different from having an indulgent father. You are your master's property. You are also the least senior in the house staff, and will be required to obey every command quickly and efficiently. If you can do this, you will be fine. If you tire easily, then life will be very, very hard for you."

Nitza swallowed hard and nodded.

"You will always refer to your master as 'Master,'" the man went on. "He has ordered that I make a bed for you in the supply closet."

"The closet?" she whispered.

"The closet," he affirmed. "I will do my best to make you comfortable. Your nights will be short. You will go to bed after the house is asleep and your work is done, and you will get up in time to light the cooking fires before dawn. You will not spend much time on your mat, I can assure you."

"My father will come for me," she said, hearing the fear in her voice. "He promised he would come."

"Your father owes our master more money than you can imagine, young lady," came the retort. "The law is on the side of our master. It will do you no good to pine away after something that will never happen. You must get used to the idea now. This is your life."

The man stopped suddenly and turned to look at her. His expression softened and he gave an apologetic shrug.

"You are young," he said gently. "But many girls are married at your age and in their husband's home. Think of that when you miss your parents. It will be difficult for you, but you will adjust. I promise you that you will get used to the work, and the ache in your heart will cease."

Tears welled up in Nitza's eyes at the man's kind words, and she struggled to control them. She felt that the lump in her throat might cut off her breath, but she forced a small smile to her lips. "I will work hard, then," she said with a quivering voice.

The man looked at her silently for a long moment. He frowned and pursed his lips, tapping his chin with one finger, then gave her a slow, sad smile.

"Nitza," he said in a low voice. "I must warn you to keep yourself busy as far away from our master as possible."

"May I ask why?" she whispered.

"There are things an unmarried girl should not know," he said simply. "And you must trust me."

Nitza's first day of work was difficult. She carried water until her shoulders ached and her arms were limp from exhaustion. Her feet were on fire, but there was no respite. As soon as one trip to the well was complete, she was sent again. When enough water had been drawn, she was set to work kneading bread dough on her knees. Batch after batch of dough passed through her hands until her knees were in agony and her already tight shoulders began to seize up.

"Faster!" a higher ranking woman snapped at her. "You aren't worth the food you consume!"

The food Nitza had been given was a pitiful amount. After she'd eaten, her stomach still rumbled with hunger, but there was no more food for her, and no more time to rest.

Despite what the steward had told her about her situation being permanent, she could not help but hope that her father would find the money to repay the loan. She dreamed that he would arrive to collect her and take her back to her mother. She thought of her father's face, of her mother's hugs, and of her home that felt so very far away.

He had promised that he would come. Even though it seemed so impossible, it seemed even more impossible for her father to break his word. He had never lied to her before. He had never failed to do what he said he would do. He would come. She knew he would come. He had to come . . . because if he didn't, she could not face the thought.

In her mind, she created the story of her father's return. Perhaps he would come in a morning when she was about to make her first trip to the well. He would arrive, take the jar from her shoulder, and pull her close to him in a hug. He would hold her while she cried.

Perhaps he would come late at night, after she had gone to bed in the closet. Perhaps he would pound on the door, awakening the entire house. He could demand the return of his daughter, and her master would have no choice but to let her go. They would walk away together, free! He would tell her that she would sleep in her own bed that night . . . that she would eat a meal that her mother had cooked for her, and that they would worship together and thank Elohim for His goodness.

Perhaps he would come midday. Tears filled her eyes. She did not have the time to work out her fantasies. They were sketchy and lacked detail. She would flesh them out when she crawled into bed, she promised herself. She would give herself the pleasure of imagining the day that her father returned for her. They might take her freedom. They might take her strength. They might take her dignity and her happiness, but they could not take her mind.

But when the night wore on, when her work was finally done and she was permitted to sleep for the very few hours until her work must start again, she could not keep her eyes open long enough to permit herself the luxury of fantasies. Sleep overtook her, and as she lay in an exhausted heap on her small mat amidst the jars, boxes, and piles of the storage closet, the chief steward looked down on her with an unreadable expression.

"She was worked hard today, sir," the steward told his master later that night. "If I might be so bold to say so, sir, she is not used to the workload, and frightening her now might bring on a bad illness. If we lost her to illness, my mistress would require a replacement, would she not?"

While Nitza slept the sleep of a worker, the steward wondered how long he could distract his master from his intended goal. And he wondered if the innocence of a serving girl was worth the trouble his meddling would likely bring onto his own head.

CHAPTER 19

HATRED WAS ALL THEY HAD

In his father's house, Zacchaeus sat with his father under the olive tree, enjoying the afternoon sun. The two men sat awkwardly together, and Zacchaeus was giving his father, who looked increasingly elderly these days, an exasperated look.

"Are you calling me a thief?" he asked in disbelief.

"I'm just asking," his father replied uncomfortably. "Do you think that is an easy question for a man to ask his son?"

"If you need me to tell you straight," Zacchaeus said, "no, I do not cheat my fellow Judeans. My fellow Judeans constantly try to hide their income."

"Your wealth," his father said. "People talk. They say that you have grown so wealthy because you cheat them, that you tell them they owe more than they do and keep the surplus for yourself."

"My wealth comes from being unmarried, having an ample income from Rome, and having no woman to spend my money out from under me," he retorted.

"You must admit," his father said, spreading his hands to show he meant no harm, "the other tax collectors are not honest or fair."

"Yes, they cheat," Zacchaeus admitted. "But the people would hate me even if they knew I was treating them honestly. I work for the Romans."

"You assist them in taxing your neighbors," his father said.

"Rome occupies Judea!" Zacchaeus exclaimed. "Can I change that? Can I bring back David to rule us? No! I have not chosen the Romans to rule us, but you must admit that Rome is our only problem. No one else seems inclined to invade us or take us off into slavery while Rome is our protector."

"Protector?" his father spat back. "They enslave us!"

"You work your own business, you head your own family, you worship your own God," Zacchaeus said. "You also walk on Roman highways."

"We do not need Romans to build our roads."

"Agreed. However, they have. They are here. So are we. They are stronger. Would you have me become a wool-headed zealot? Would you have me sacrifice my life in a scuffle in a street to prove a point? Must I curse them over my meal and sour the meat in my stomach for an ideal? This is the lot Elohim gave us. If we are to be delivered, then He must send the Messiah and do so."

Zacchaeus threw his hands in the air and turned away, trying to calm his anger. It was an old argument, one that would never be resolved.

"You are to be married soon," his father said, his voice more gentle. "We should not be fighting at a happy time like this."

Zacchaeus gave his father an amused look.

"Will you ever say things the way they really are?" he asked, but there was laughter in his voice. "Yes, I will be married very soon."

"Have you heard from the ones you invited?" his father asked.

He had heard. That morning servants from various households—even one not invited—came by with their master's regrets.

"My master cannot come," one had said. "It is a very busy time for his business and he cannot be away."

"My master has sent his regrets," another had said. "His mother has become ill and he does not want to leave her."

"My master apologizes, but he cannot come," still another had said. "He has a terribly sore leg."

The regrets kept coming, all morning long. Apparently, all of Yericho was in terrible straights the night of Zacchaeus' wedding, and would be wallowing in sadness and misery while he was joined for life to the widow Tzofit. It was oddly appropriate.

"I have heard from many guests," Zacchaeus said. "Have you heard from the guests that you invited, Father?"

His father cleared his throat and looked away.

"They will not come," Zacchaeus said, not needing the answer.

"No, son, they had some very strange events, it seems . . ."

Zacchaeus let out a bitter laugh and shook his head.

"They hate me," he said. "I know it. They hated me when I was a child because I would not grow. They hated me when I was a boy, when I was a youth, and when I became a man. And now they hate me still, but they say it is because I am a tax collector."

"I'm sorry, son," his father said, raising sad eyes to meet his son's. "I know how much you wanted a proper wedding celebration."

"And I'll have it!"

"Without guests?"

"There *will* be guests," Zacchaeus replied. "There will be magnificent food, delightful entertainment, and dancing. It will be the most tasteful, elegant wedding celebration ever to be held in Yericho. Unfortunately, all of Yericho's finest are occupied with sick mothers, dying cows, failing businesses, and illnesses of the stomach. So I shall invite others . . . Yericho's second best. And third best. There will be guests, Father! Trust me, there will be guests."

Zacchaeus pushed himself to his feet and looked sadly down at his father.

"You have two more days until you are a married man," his father said in an attempt at merriment. "What will you do with yourself?"

"Rumor has it that Yeshua the healer is coming through Yericho tomorrow," Zacchaeus said. "In my last treasured moments as a bachelor, I would like to see that magnificent healer. While I may not have distinguished guests to celebrate my dismal marriage, I will at least try to see greatness as it passes by me."

"Some say the healer is the Messiah," his father commented.

"May Elohim give Him strength to restore Israel," Zacchaeus said. "For your sake, at least, Father."

When the Messiah did come, what place would there be for pragmatists like himself?

Tzofit lay in her bed. She was not a maiden, uncertain of what marriage would hold. Her husband was not a stranger to her. She could not lie here this night wondering what he would look like, or what wonderful attributes he would have. She knew the man she would be given to the next evening. She knew him well, and she could not stomach him.

The night before her marriage to Oshri, her mother had sat with her, combing her long hair.

"They say he'll come tomorrow night," her mother had said. "And you'll be a married woman, my little Tzofit."

"Is he nice?" she had asked.

"Very," her mother replied. "And he is handsome. Very kind to his mother, they say. You can tell if a man is a good man by how he treats his mother."

Tzofit had been silent, her stomach in knots. What would happen? She knew that she would be alone with her husband, but what would happen behind those doors, she did not know. What would marriage be like? It all seemed so adult and far away, somehow, yet tomorrow it would be her life.

"You are nervous," her mother had said. "Don't worry. I will give you some advice."

Tzofit had turned to look her mother in the face. Gray now streaked her mother's black hair. Her face was plump and laugh lines surrounded her dark eyes. Tzofit felt tears rising up when she realized that tomorrow would be her last day with her mother.

"Marriage is about duty," her mother said. "You have a role you must perform. You must clean and cook, bear children, and obey your husband. If you perform your role well, then you will be happy enough, regardless of what kind of man your husband is. A good wife has nothing to do with whether her husband is good or not."

"So if I behave myself properly . . ." Tzofit said, a question in her voice. "But is marriage ever truly happy?"

"Oh, it can be!" her mother said, leaning forward and lowering her voice. "For a wonderful experience as a wife, you must do more. You must find his heart and cradle it. If you can arouse genuine affection in his heart, you will be a blissful wife, indeed."

"Did you find Father's heart?" Tzofit whispered.

"I did," her mother said with a knowing smile. "I did."

And then she had stood, kissed Tzofit tenderly on the forehead, and turned to leave the room.

"Rest, dearest," she had said. "You will need your rest for tomorrow evening."

For years during her marriage to Oshri, Tzofit had wondered about her mother's mysterious advice. But try as she might, all she could do was perform her role. Her husband was a mystery to her and his heart was the furthest thing from her reach. Soon, even being a good wife in spite of him began to be impossible. Now she was about to be married to her dead husband's brother, and her mother's advice seemed to be entirely unattainable . . . yet again.

Zacchaeus. He was to be her husband! She let out a bitter laugh as tears welled up in her eyes.

"Oh, Elohim," she whispered. "Have I not been punished enough? I was not the wife I should have been to Oshri, but be merciful to me. Do not punish me further with his horrible brother."

Tonight, there was no comforting hand to comb her hair. There was no womanly advice to be given for her to lean on and believe in. There was no one to tell her that this was a happy time and that she should rejoice, even though her heart was breaking. She was alone, lying in the bed she used to share with her late husband. She was alone, praying to Elohim to work a miracle to rival the parting of the Red Sea, and stop this miserable marriage from going through.

Tzofit was alone, realizing that by this time the next night, she would be joined to a man she hated, a man who despised her. She would be married to a man that no one else respected, yet whom she must respect and obey. She would be married to the brother-in-law she used to comfort herself with by saying, "Oshri might be bad, but at least I'm not married to his brother!"

As the dusk passed into night, Tzofit lay on her bed sobbing softly to herself. No one heard her cry. No one, that is, but her mother-in-law who crept quietly by and pretended not to hear.

In a low-ranking Roman Legionary's home that night, the lamps were blazing and the wine flowing. Busts of the hosts' long dead family members were arranged along one wall in a monument to family history, giving the feeling that these silent ancestors looked gravely down on the meal. Servants in belted, white tunics moved between guests, their muscular arms hoisting dishes and jugs of wine, and conversation buzzed through the air like lazy flies on a hot summer's day. One long, low table was surrounded by reclining guests. Heaped high on the table were beds of lettuce with tuna fish, and sliced eggs topped by strong leeks. Nearly empty were the bowls of spiced chickpeas, pale beans with bacon, and sausages served over white grits, and the servants whisked the platters away to be replaced by green cabbage, bread, and fish sauce. Dishes of dried grapes, fresh pears, and roasted Neopolitan chestnuts were not far behind. Through it all, the wine kept flowing.

Clodia looked over at her husband who was leaning close to another man in animated conversation. It had been a long time since Gaius had taken her to a dinner. Many times the dinners were for men only, and at other dinners that he never spoke of, she knew that other women sat in her rightful place. But tonight, she accompanied her husband as the legal wife. This was an important dinner, one that her husband hoped would help him to climb to a higher position in the military, and therefore he was obligated to present his most respectable side—his wife.

Clodia raised her glass for more wine, enjoying the heady buzz she already had from the evening's alcohol.

"My dear friends," the host's voice rang out. "I am so glad that you have come to eat with me tonight. The gods have smiled on me to grant me such company, I am sure."

There was a smattering of clapping as people turned their heads toward their host. No meal was a free meal, and they were about to pay for their food.

"Tonight, for your delightful entertainment, I would like to present something rather . . . personal." He hung his head bashfully for several theatrical moments, then raised his glowing face to look at the people before him.

"I have written a ballad," he said. "A small thing, but I do hope that you appreciate my humble dance with the muse."

"A small thing, indeed!" one of the women close by whispered. "I know for a fact that he's been working on that ballad for months."

Clodia could not help but smirk. Their host was known to be rather long winded, and while his dinners had the most wonderful fare around, they were also the longest . . . not because of the revelry of the guests, but because of the poetry publishing of the host.

"I have written on a subject dear to our hearts . . . of Rome. Sweet, beautiful mother to us all. I write of war, of valor, of protecting the nation that sprung out of the farmlands of the seven hills."

"His topic can't be argued with," Clodia whispered back.

"But his rhythm and storytelling certainly can be," came the retort, and Clodia covered a laugh behind her hand.

"It was his duty to feed and entertain us," Clodia said. "And it is our duty to endure as much as possible before we claim exhaustion—or drink ourselves into stupors."

The other woman raised her glass for more wine and gave Clodia a wink. "If I must go down," she said dramatically, "I go down with the finest of wine."

"Straight under the table!" her husband beside her snapped with a baleful look. She returned his glare coolly and took a sip from her glass.

Clodia knew her duty. She was duty bound to her husband to help him rise politically. She was duty bound to her host, to make him feel important by politely listening to his amateur poetry. She was duty bound to her family to show her finest side. But she was owed something, too. She was owed a fine meal, limitless wine, and the position she held as wife of a centurion and a part of the familiar assembly of people of similar social level. She would take what was owed to her, like the woman to her left.

Clodia glanced toward Gaius who had ceased his conversation and had plastered a look of interest on his face as the host commenced his lengthy poem. The host stood with his toga arranged artfully around him and one hand raised up to the rooftop, his eyes cast upward and his lips trembling with emotion.

"So he begins . . ." the woman beside Clodia whispered.

And so he did. He continued the pleasure of publishing his poetry for the next two and a half hours.

As Clodia sat, swallowing yawns and pretending interest, she realized that she had been given all that was owed to her. She was a wife. She was wealthy. She was part of a comfortable social stratus. She was well dressed and entertained. She had received her due. It was a sad thought, really, because her due was not enough. There was much that was missing. Her eyes cut in the direction of her husband and looking at him, the deep loathing bubbled back up inside of her. She could not forgive him. She would not forgive him. He had taken her baby from her, taken her heart right out of her chest, and she would never, as long as she breathed, forget her hatred for her husband.

Sometimes, it seemed, that a dinner was all a person had left to hold onto.

CHAPTER 20

It's About Duty

Ehud stared at the wall of his home, seeing nothing. His hair was limp and uncombed. He held his beard in one hand, clinging to it as if it could save him. His skin was pale and dark circles ringed his eyes.

His wife could not look at him. "Where is she now?" she asked woodenly.

"She has been taken into Seth's house as a servant," he replied.

"For how long?"

"I don't know."

"Is she treated kindly?" Her voice was desperately. "She is not used to serving. She might displease them, Ehud. She might displease them!"

Ehud knew what his wife meant. She was thinking of beatings, punishments, cruelties. Nitza was a slave. She was a piece of property. He shuddered at the thought. He could not allow his mind to imagine it. The thought of his daughter being subjected to lashes or even slaps, was too much for him right now.

"Oh, Elohim!" he prayed aloud. "God of my fathers. Oh, Elohim, my child has been taken from me. Help us! Oh, Elohim, help us to get her back."

His voice cracked into a sob.

"How much do you owe?" she asked quietly.

"Enough," he replied. Exact figures were not for women to know. The exact figure was too humiliating to say.

"How will you repay it?" she asked.

He was silent.

"We cannot leave Nitza with that man!" she cried, her voice shrill. "We cannot! Husband, she is only a child!"

"She is nearly old enough to marry." He wasn't sure why he said it.

"Is she old enough to be enslaved? Is she old enough to be sold on the market, used like an animal, and taken from us forever?"

"No, no . . ." he moaned. "She is not. She does not deserve to pay for my stupidity."

"Then what do we do? What do we do? What can I do?"

But it wasn't Dassah's job to do something to save their daughter. It was his. It was his responsibility to rescue his child. He was the man. He was the provider, the protector. He was supposed to be the answer.

"I offered myself in her place," Ehud said, tears slipping down his cheeks and melting into his beard. "I offered myself! I can work harder. I could be of more value. But he would not take me . . ."

"Yourself?" Dassah whispered. "But husband, what would become of us without you?"

"What has become of you with me?"

They were silent, the house heavy, dark, and quiet like a tomb. To lose a child to death seemed like less of a blow than to lose her to a life of misery and slavery. At least the community would mourn with them for a death. But this? They would blame him. As he blamed himself. As his wife likely blamed him, too.

"I know of only one man who has enough money to pay this debt," he said after a moment.

"Who?" she asked, frowning.

"Zacchaeus, the tax collector."

"You know him?" she asked, surprised. "How? Why would he help you?"

"Don't ask," he snapped. "But he has the resources."

"And what do you have to offer in return for the money?"

"Only myself, dear wife," he said, his voice quivering. "Only myself."

"Offer me, also," Dassah said, her grief-stricken eyes meeting her husband's. "My future is bound to yours."

Merav, after receiving the invitation to his wedding dinner, thought of Zacchaeus daily, and she wondered if he also thought of her. This was why, the day that Zacchaeus was to be united with his widowed sister-in-law, Merav stood brazenly in front of the door to his home, her breath caught in her throat, and her hand raised to knock.

Before she could knock, however, the door opened and she stood in stunned silence, face to face with an equally stunned Zacchaeus.

"Merav!" he said in surprise.

She dipped her head and swallowed hard.

A warm smile lit his face. "Please, come inside," he said. "I have been thinking of you. Well, truthfully, I was wondering why I had not heard from you about my invitation."

"Ah," she said quietly, dry-washing her knobby hands in front of her. "Well, I don't know what to say, really . . ."

"That you will come, I hope," he said earnestly. "I have few enough sincere friends."

She looked at him, at his anxious eyes and his pretended nonchalance. He cared for her, she realized in a rush. She did not know in what way, but he certainly cared for her.

"I came to talk to you, Zacchaeus," she said slowly. "I must say what I have to say now, before my bravery fails me."

"You, dear woman, are braver than a suicidal zealot," he retorted with a laugh, and she could not help but bark out a laugh with him.

"You make me happy, Zacchaeus," she said, still chuckling.

"And you warm my heart, as well." He gestured for her to sit down. "Now tell me, my friend, what is on your mind?"

Merav sat down on the chair indicated and closed her eyes, willing the shaking of her limbs to cease. She had never felt more terror in her life. It was a strange feeling for a woman who had always faced life like a lion, roaring in its face.

"I have a business proposition," she said finally.

"Today, of all days?" he asked in surprise.

"It cannot wait," she said, looking pleadingly at him. "Please, hear me out."

"Of course, I will," he said, frowning thoughtfully. "Go on."

"I have a plot of land," she said. "It is next to your family land, and if the two were to be put together, they would be a beautiful property, indeed. Quite valuable, I believe. More valuable than they are separately."

"Hmm," he said.

"This land was my dowry, and it is mine again, now that my husband is dead," she explained. "My family wants to remarry me to an older man who needs a nursemaid. They want to dispose of me, while keeping my property in the family."

"I see," he said. "And where do I come in?"

Merav was silent, summoning up her courage to speak her heart. Zacchaeus looked back at her, his eyes meeting hers levelly.

"I would like to join our properties," she said finally.

"You would sell it to me?" he asked. "Would your family agree to the sale?"

"No," she said simply. "They would not. But they might agree to a marriage."

Now that the words were out, she stared at him, her lips clamped together in a straight line and her breath coming shakily through her nose. She looked down at her thin, long legs and long feet, willing herself to breath, but refusing to look up.

"A marriage between us?" he asked slowly.

She was silent, and so was he. She stole a look in his direction and saw him standing with his arms crossed over his chest, deep in thought. He hadn't rejected her outright.

"It would not be an ordinary marriage, and people would likely talk," she said quietly. "But no more than they do already, I imagine. I don't know that our relationship would be traditional, either, but we would be company for each other. We would understand and support each other. We could talk over splendid meals late into the night . . ."

Something wistful and heartrending passed over his face at the mention of late dinners, and she stopped speaking.

"You know I am to go collect my bride tonight," he said at last.

"Yes, but you are a man, if you put off the day for a week, you will be forgiven," she said. "If you wanted time to consider . . ."

He turned to her, his eyes brimming with unshed tears. He was standing, looking down at her seated before him. Seated the way she was, she could even imagine that he was of natural height . . . and that she was young again.

"We would have a union of rare affection and wonderful dinners," he said, his voice quivering ever so slightly. "We would, Merav . . ."

"But?" she whispered.

"My family has arranged a wedding for me." He shook his head slowly. "I do not want to marry Tzofit, but since when has marriage been about our desires and wishes? It is about family. It is about unity. It is about duty."

"Perhaps they would reconsider," she offered weakly.

"There are extenuating circumstances," he said with a wave of his hand. "My happiness must be sacrificed for the family."

She nodded, looking back down to her lap. She took a deep breath. Let it out.

"I'm sorry," Zacchaeus said softly.

Life must be faced like a lion, roaring in its face. She steeled herself and stood up. She had done what she had come to do. She had received her answer.

As Zacchaeus watched Merav walk resolutely away from his home, her long limbs carrying her with the grace of a loping camel, he realized sadly that it was likely he would never see his friend again. Not in the same way, at least, not after a discussion like the one they had just had. Discussions of marriage, whether the marriages happened or not, had a way of changing relationships permanently.

The morning sun was bright and sparkled against the sandy ground. It still hung low in the sky, its rays still golden and gentle. He stood in the door to his home, looking out at the Yericho streets with a heavy heart.

What he hadn't told Merav was that he wished he had a choice in his marriage. He wished that changing their minds was an option. He wished that he could face his days with the quirky, interesting, compassionate Merav, eating fine dinners, laughing together over the day's events. It would not be a traditional marriage relationship. Children would not be attempted, obviously, at her age. But there would be companionship he could trust. There would be witty conversation. There would be someone waiting for him when he came home . . . someone who liked him, possibly even loved him in her own way. He would no longer be alone.

Zacchaeus desperately wished that he could have said yes.

But the sun was shining, and the day was ahead of him. He had duties to perform today. He had duties that he could not shirk. And one of those duties was to marry his sister-in-law, Tzofit.

CHAPTER 21

THE QUESTION

Her few belongings packed in sacks, Tzofit now stood in her room, looking about. It was foolishness, really. Normally, when a widow was passed to the deceased brother, her living arrangements would not change. Yet here she was, preparing to be escorted to her new husband's home as if she were a maid of 13 again.

Looking down at the bed she had shared with Oshri brought back a flood of memories. She recalled being brought there as a new wife filled with fear and anxiety. She recalled her struggles to be the wife her husband's family wanted her to be, but they had all wanted something different from her. The role of wife she had been taught by her mother didn't seem to be the answer. Her mother-in-law expected obedience and compliance. Her father-in-law seemed to expect her to stand up like a woman and carry herself with the very dignity that would irritate her mother-in-law most. Her brother-in-law seemed to find her amusing at best, and her husband seemed to have very few expectations, indeed.

Oshri. She wanted to blame him, but now that he had died and could no longer fight her, she found herself unable to. He had been her husband. She had been his wife. She remembered his beard that seemed to reach his eyebrows, his laughing eyes, and his petulant lips. She remembered him with his tentative overtures toward her when he wanted to be husbandly, and she remembered her anger and spite toward his weaknesses. It all seemed so pitiful now. Why hadn't she seen it then? He had not been able to be what she wanted him to be, but was that so wrong?

She moved toward the small window and looked out at the day. The sun was high in the sky, washing out the bright greens of foliage and the vibrant patterns of people's clothing into a pastel palate. The sky was a pale blue with a few stringy clouds whisping across its surface. Today was a day she would remember. Today was the end of something.

"Oh, Oshri," she whispered. "I'm sorry."

And she was sorry. She was sorry that she hadn't loved him more when he was still living. She was sorry that she hadn't appreciated the things that she now found herself inexplicably missing about him . . . his laughing eyes, his meek smile, his questioning attempts at tenderness.

There was a tap on her door, and she looked up to see her mother-in-law standing awkwardly outside.

"Elohim be with you, Mother," Tzofit said quietly.

"And with you," Shahar replied. She cleared her throat and stepped into the room.

"I have packed," Tzofit said, nodding to the few bags of clothing. "Only my clothing and a few trinkets from my mother, and from Oshri. I didn't think you would mind my taking Oshri's gifts to me."

"No, no," Shahar said, shaking her head. "Not at all. They are yours."

They were silent together for a moment.

"Tonight you will be married," Shahar said.

"Yes."

"I will not pretend that it is happy for you," Shahar said in a low voice.

"But I am provided for, and for that I am thankful," Tzofit said graciously. This was not a time to complain, especially when complaints would not change reality.

"I am glad to hear you say it," Shahar said, looking relieved. "I meant to do well by you, you know."

Tzofit did not know how to respond to this. Her mother-in-law had never been kind or compassionate. She had never been understanding or even showed much evidence of liking her.

"To give you to my second son speaks of you, you know," Shahar said feebly. They both knew that she was lying.

Tzofit fingered the sleeves of her robe. She hadn't dressed yet for her wedding procession, but her clothes were laid out and waiting. Some jewels had also been set aside: a jeweled chain for her forehead, some bangles for her wrists, some bells for her ankles, and a small assortment of rings. Her father-in-law had provided for her, picked the articles out himself, apparently.

"I thought that perhaps I could . . . speak as a mother," Shahar offered. "Since you will be married soon."

Tzofit shivered. "If you would like to."

Shahar cleared her throat and looked down at her fidgeting hands.

"Marriage is not easy," she said quietly. "As you know. Pleasing a man is hard. Pleasing his mother is harder still."

Tzofit glanced up at her mother-in-law in surprise, but Shahar still stood looking down at her hands.

"I know that Zacchaeus is not your choice in a husband," she said. "I know that the two of you have your differences . . . and that he might not be . . . physically what a woman would want . . ."

Her voice trailed away as if saying this was painful for her. She took a deep breath and continued.

"I made mistakes with Oshri," she said. "I coddled him too much. I favored him. I never made him leave my skirts. I know that now, and I know that being married to such a son would be . . . tiresome."

Shahar looked up at Tzofit, her face strained and her eyes sad.

"I miss him, Tzofit," she said with a quiver in her voice. "He was my son, and he loved me. Of everyone in my life, he loved me."

"I know," Tzofit replied.

"But Zacchaeus is different. He is stronger than Oshri. He doesn't listen to my advice and little cares about my opinions. It is not easy as a mother with such a son, but it will be better for you as a wife."

Shahar cleared her throat again, then awkwardly reached out to pat Tzofit's arm, pulling away when she felt her daughter-in-law's tensed muscles.

"Would you like assistance in dressing?" she asked tentatively.

Tzofit looked at the dress and the jewels. She looked at the soft sandals and the veil to cover her head. She would need assistance in preparing for her wedding. It was not a task a woman could accomplish alone, no matter how much she might wish to have solitude.

"Yes, Mother," Tzofit said quietly. "I would appreciate that."

Dressing for her wedding night could be put off no longer.

"Tzofit" meant "She is watching," and Shahar thought that her daughter-in-law's name was appropriate. Tzofit was always watching. Those eyes trailed after Shahar as she walked through the courtyard. They followed her as she bent over the bread, kneading the dough in a soft mound. They followed her as she knelt before her husband, offering refreshments, and they followed her as she tried to get a moment's solitude to think. There was no solitude. Tzofit was always watching.

The city watched, too. They'd watched when Zacchaeus was born, and they judged. They watched as he grew up, and they continued to judge. And they watched now as he was about to marry. The city had eyes . . . eyes everywhere that were evaluating and judging. It was her constant fear that they would see it . . . that their idle gossip would strike on the truth.

Her two sons never did look alike. It was not only their height. It was everything from their mannerisms to their faces. They were as different as sheep and doves. Oshri had been much like his father in appearance. He was hairy. He was tall. He had that way of fluttering his fingers when he talked and felt uncertain. Oshri was obviously his father's son. Zacchaeus, however . . . Zacchaeus was like his mother. He was solid. He was resolute. He was stubborn. He looked nothing like Chayim, and there was a good reason for that.

When Shahar was pregnant with Oshri, Chayim had borrowed a great deal of money from a new moneylender, Seth Ben Isaac. Chayim's brother had gotten himself into a great deal of debt and was about to be imprisoned. Chayim couldn't watch his own brother thrown into a dungeon, and so he did what any good brother would do. He found the money. Paying it back, however, proved more difficult than he'd thought, and Shahar watched her husband wracked by worry. She did not know how much her husband owed, but she knew that it must be a very large amount, and that terrified her.

It was then that Seth Ben Isaac had made his suggestion. If Shahar would submit to him, he would forgive her husband's debt and Chayim would never have to know. At first Shahar had refused. Then she had started to wonder. Would it be so terrible if it saved her family? Was her modesty and purity worth a lifetime of imprisonment for her husband and a life of begging for her child? Who was she to stand upon principle when much larger things were at stake? And so she had decided in her heart to agree. Not only would she agree, but she would offer Seth exactly what he wanted. Her husband need never know. Before she had the opportunity, Chayim came up with the money. It hadn't been so much, after all. Seth had been lying. And Shahar's purity remained intact . . . or did it? She *would* have. She would have done it, and she knew that as surely as she knew that she breathed.

"Mother," Tzofit said quietly.

Shahar adjusted Tzofit's robe and smoothed the fabric belt through her fingers.

"I am not a good wife," Tzofit said quietly.

Shahar considered this for a long moment.

"We all have our weaknesses," she said finally. "None of us are quite so good as we appear."

"Zacchaeus is not wicked like they say," Shahar said suddenly. "He is not wicked!"

Tzofit nodded, and Shahar clamped her mouth shut. She had already said too much.

Zacchaeus held a package in one hand and fished in his money-bag for a penny. The woman stood before him with her bread, watching his hand hungrily, waiting for a coin to appear. She licked her lips nervously and he noticed her look around herself several times during their interaction as if she were afraid of being watched.

"Give me two, miss," he said, gesturing toward her loaves.

"Yes, sir," she said, pulling another loaf from her sack, her eyes still on the pennies in his hand. He dropped them into her palm, and they immediately disappeared into a fold in her threadbare robe.

"He's coming! Someone saw him!" a voice not far away said excitedly.

"Really?

"Now?"

"Yes!"

"He's not far off! He's coming this way!"

Voices around him grew shrill and excited, and Zacchaeus looked at the bread seller with raised eyebrows.

"Who is coming this way?" he asked.

She looked at him in alarm. She swallowed and looked around again.

"Who?" he repeated.

"It must be the healer," she said quickly. "Yeshua from Nazareth. They said he would come today."

"Really!" Zacchaeus exclaimed, turning to look in the direction that the crowd was moving. He needed to get home soon to prepare to fetch his bride, but a chance to see someone so talked about, so distinguished did not come along every day.

The crowd grew quickly as people began to angle in the direction that Yeshua was said to be moving. Zacchaeus hated crowds. They boxed him in and he could never see over all the shoulders to what everyone else saw. Now people were flooding toward him, and while he first mentally debated heading in the opposite direction, Zacchaeus suddenly felt a flood of excitement.

"I've got to see him!" Zacchaeus said, turning impulsively toward the bread seller. "Do you realize what a chance this is?"

She blinked at him and he muttered something in disgust about the lower classes and their levels of intelligence. The crowd pushed in further and as Zacchaeus stood on his tiptoes and looked around, disappointment came crushing down on him. He could see nothing but shoulders and heads and waving arms.

"There he is!" the woman cried, her face suddenly lit with joy. "I see him!"

Zacchaeus looked in the direction she was looking, but the bodies pressing around him blocked his vision. He strained to stretch taller and a veil flittered across his face.

"Look!" a boy cried out. "Shem, let's go climb that wall!"

It was pathetic that Zacchaeus was having the exact problem that the schoolboys were having. It was pathetic that a low class woman could see more than he could. It was pathetic that on the day of his marriage, when Zacchaeus was supposed to be celebrating, he felt that the high point of his day was to see a traveling healer. But as he watched the boys scramble up the wall, he could not help but think of he and Oshri. If they were boys again, Oshri would have raced him to the nearest tree and leaped up its trunk. If they were teens together again, Oshri would have still raced him to the nearest tree, and he would have pointed out the prettiest girl on his way.

Someone pushed against him, and Zacchaeus stumbled backward, his foot catching against a root, sending him sprawling. Cursing under his breath, Zacchaeus pushed himself back up onto his feet, his eyes looking up into the limbs of the sycamore tree. No one was watching him. Everyone was looking in the opposite direction, down the street toward Yeshua who seemed to be making slow progress because of the press of the crowd. There were cries of

"Please, bless my baby," and "Master! Heal me!" and Zacchaeus wondered momentarily if he was crazy for what he was about to do. But he didn't wonder for long. He reached up, grabbed the first limb, and swung himself up.

As he pulled himself up into the branches, Zacchaeus laughed out loud. Grown men did not climb trees, but for once on this dismal day, something would go his way. He wanted to see the healer with his own eyes, and by all that was good and righteous, he would see the healer. He was a man. He would have his way in something.

As Zacchaeus looked down, he remembered this view. He remembered being a boy, looking down at the girls who passed by on their way for water. He remembered giggling with his brother, their goading each other on to braver and braver heights. He remembered the feeling of the tree bark against his legs, the feeling of the wind against his face, the feeling of his feet dangling down into the air, and he ruefully recalled his youthful arrogance, calling down to the tanner's daughter that she was beautiful.

The crowd had grown denser still, and Zacchaeus mentally congratulated himself on his quick decision. While people milled in frustration, standing up on tiptoes to see, he could see over the heads of everyone. And suddenly, there He was. Zacchaeus spotted Yeshua moving slowly, reaching out to touch children and beggars, men and women, as He walked.

He could tell his grandchildren of this day. The thought shocked him as quickly as it entered his mind. He would be married. He would have children. He would have grandchildren! It was a strangely exhilarating thought. Today, as he sat hidden in a tree, he would witness miracles that he would tell his grandchildren about.

Yeshua was coming closer. Now Zacchaeus could make out His face. He wasn't what Zacchaeus expected. He had kind eyes, a dark beard. He had a ready smile and a laugh that carried, but He didn't look royal. He didn't look Messianic, if Zacchaeus even knew what that would look like. But even from that distance he could see that Yeshua had charisma, and people were drawn to Him. In a surprising, unexpected way, Zacchaeus felt drawn to Him too.

Now Yeshua had come closer. He was almost beneath the sycamore tree where Zacchaeus sat, and the small man pulled his feet up, afraid that a dangling sandal might draw attention into the tree. As he did, Yeshua looked away from a child He was talking to and

His eyes moved upward. Zacchaeus froze. This was not what he'd planned. This was not what he wanted. He had imagined Yeshua walking on beneath him, moving away, and leaving him with a memory of greatness passing on the dusty road below. But instead, Yeshua stopped, shaded His eyes, and looked straight up into the branches of the tree.

Zacchaeus stared back in mute horror. He could hear the spattering of laughter. He could see the people pointing and shaking their heads, and he felt the heat of shame rising up in his face.

"Zacchaeus!" Yeshua called.

He looked down in stunned silence.

"Zacchaeus!" Yeshua repeated. "That is your name, isn't it?"

"Yes . . . yes . . ." he stammered.

"Come down here, Zacchaeus," Yeshua said.

Zacchaeus felt the scrape of bark against his skin as he slid down from his perch. As his feet hit the ground, he was shamefully aware of his diminutive stature as he looked up into the Yeshua's face.

"My friend," Yeshua said, clapping him on the back and gripping his shoulder. "I must dine with you tonight!"

The laughter and mocking in the crowd turned to whispers of shock and envy. Zacchaeus blinked, wondering if he had heard properly.

"Master?" Zacchaeus said in a low voice.

"I must dine with you," Yeshua repeated, his warm eyes meeting Zacchaeus' gaze levelly. "Will you have me?"

"Yes!" Zacchaeus laughed out loud. "Yes! Of course I will have you! Of course!"

"Walk with me," Yeshua said.

And the living, writhing, moving crowd propelled them forward, toward Zacchaeus' home and his upcoming wedding dinner.

CHAPTER 22

SURVIVAL

Nitza's arms were burning as she hoisted the water jar onto her shoulders. It was empty, but it might as well have been filled to the brim for all the strength she had. She was exhausted. She had slept horribly the night before, finally crying herself to sleep from loneliness for her parents, only to be awoken before dawn by the steward. It was time to start her day.

Now, as she prepared go on her fifth trip to the well for water, her arms quivered under the effort of the work. She wished she could break down and cry, but she knew that the tears would take even more of her limited strength and she couldn't afford to waste her energy.

Two of the other serving girls, whispering nearby, glanced at her uneasily. She looked back at them questioningly.

"Is it true?" one of the girls asked.

"Is what true?" Nitza asked.

"Are you being sold?"

Nitza blinked. She hadn't heard anything about it, but that didn't mean it wasn't true. Her heart dropped.

"I hadn't heard!" Nitza said truthfully. "Where did you hear?"

"Just around," the second girl said, shrugging apologetically. "I heard that the master tired of your obstinacy, and that he was going to sell you."

"My obstinacy?" Nitza asked, tears rising in her eyes. "I work hard! I don't complain! I work!"

"It's not the work," the older girl said with a knowing laugh. "It's what you won't do besides work. You do realize that if the master were more pleased with you, you wouldn't have to work half so hard as you do, don't you?"

No, Nitza did not know that. But as she made her way to the well, a commonly known truth about the way the world worked began to dawn on her. Her master wanted something from her . . .

153

something that she should not give, but something that had value enough to give her some power. She had been avoiding the master's attention based both on the steward's warning and her own instinct that the man's interest in her was not strictly pure. But had she gone too far? Would the master sell her?

The thought stayed in her head the whole day, and when her chores were done and she was allowed to go to eat her small portion with the other serving girls, she decided that the rules had changed. She was no longer a girl at home under the protection of her father. The worst thing that could happen to her at home with her father was now nothing compared to what could happen to her as a slave. The worst thing she could now think of was to be sold . . . sent away to another, possibly cruel master, where her father would never find her again.

So when she could have been taking her meager rest with the other serving girls, instead she asked in the kitchen for a cup of watered wine.

"What for?" the cook demanded.

"The master," Nitza said boldly.

The cook shrugged, poured the wine, and sent her back out. It was easy enough, and not entirely a lie. The master had not asked for wine, but she would bring it to him regardless. She would steel herself for whatever loathsome thing he had in mind for her with those leering eyes, and she would do what she must.

She found the master in his sitting room, lounging on pillows. His robes were up around his knees and his bare legs, white with dark hair, were exposed. He was alone, a cup of wine in one hand and some scrolls in front of him, one lying on his large belly. Scraps of food lay next to him on a platter, half eaten and greasy. Nitza stood in the doorway for several moments, waiting to be noticed, but when he didn't look up, she stepped quietly into the room. His eyes lifted and rested on her.

"What is it?" he demanded.

She didn't know what to say she had come for. She didn't know how to put it into words, or how to even hint about it. It was wicked, she knew. It was against the laws of Elohim, she was positive, and no part of her wanted to do it, but she was here to do it anyway. She was here to do what she must.

"Well?" he said.

Nitza cleared here throat and stepped forward, proffering the wine in front of her, her eyes submissively cast downward. He looked at the wine in his hand, and then to the wine she offered.

"I have wine," he said, annoyed.

"I have brought more," she whispered in her fear.

He grunted, took it from her hand, put it down on the floor close by him, and turned back to his scrolls, giving her no more notice than a piece of furniture.

Nitza was confused. She didn't know what had changed. Why were his eyes no longer following her? Why did he no longer have that funny, lazy look about him when he watched her? Why had he lost interest?

She turned to leave, but as she did, the steward walked into the room. He looked at her, his eyes boring into her until she positively glowed with shame. He could see it in her, she knew. He knew why she was here in this room, even if her master did not. She looked away, humiliated to be caught in this moment.

"Master," the steward said, "you called for me?"

"I did," the master said. "Do you see that one?"

He gestured with his chin in Nitza's direction where she bent picking up the platter of table scraps. The steward's eyes moved toward her again, rested on her for an agonizing moment, then turned back to the master.

"Yes," he said.

"There is a buyer for her, isn't there?" Again impatience filled his voice.

"Yes, sir," the steward said. "Good money he's offering, too."

"Arrange it, then," the master said. "As soon as possible."

Nitza felt her stomach leap to her throat and the room spun for a moment.

"He will come back through Yericho in a few days," the steward said, no emotion showing in his voice.

"Good. Complete the transaction." And with a flick of his finger the two were dismissed.

As they walked away, leaving their master in peace, the steward looked down at Nitza.

"Why were you there?" he asked quietly.

Nitza could not reply.

"It is not worth it, little one," the steward said sadly. "I know what you were trying to do, and I know that you think the sacrifice is worth staying here."

A lump had risen in Nitza's throat, and she blinked back the tears that threatened to overwhelm her.

"You are too naïve to know what you would be sacrificing, and what you would be required to actually do," he said, shaking his head. "And I am glad that you failed."

She hung her head, silent and humiliated.

"You will be sold, Nitza," he said quietly. "But it is to your credit. You are a good girl, and you must not let anything change that. The place you are going is far away, but the master is fair and as far as I know, he would not expect you to do the loathsome things that this master would expect of you."

"But my father . . ." Nitza whispered.

"Don't put your hope in the impossible," the steward said sadly. "It hurts too much when your dreams are dashed. Trust me on that. I know."

Benyamin had been so certain. He had known, *known* that it was the right thing to do. He had felt it as surely as he had been breathing. He had felt it in the rhythm of his own heartbeat. Zacchaeus stood for everything vile and loathsome in Judean society. He represented everything that Benyamin hated: selfishness, betrayal, dishonesty, disloyalty, sin. Zacchaeus was all these things and more. He sold his own people to the Romans! He aided the Romans in taxing the society they dominated. Benyamin had been so certain that killing Zacchaeus was the righteous thing to do.

"Have there been any advances, Benyamin?"

The group was meeting again in the same shabby space. The air was laden with the smell of their sweat and breath and they leaned forward on their elbows, facing each other earnestly. Time was of the essence.

"There has been," Benyamin said slowly. "I know that Zacchaeus is to be married tonight. I know that his illustrious guests refused to come. I know that his wedding feast will be attended by commoners, so I would not look out of sorts in the least. I could slip in easily."

"Then it is planned?" one man pressed. "Tonight he dies?"

Benyamin was silent.

"Are you wavering, brother?"

"I am not wavering!" Benyamin snapped. "I am loyal to Judah and Elohim!"

"You do not look committed," the old man said, his voice high and reedy over the other deeper voices of younger men.

"I . . ." Benyamin stopped.

"You are weakening," another said. "It was your idea, Benyamin. You saw the opportunity to strike at the heart of Rome's stranglehold on this people. Why do you waver now?"

"The idea is sound," Benyamin said. "It is good. It is righteous, is it not?" He looked around for confirmation. The men nodded and grunted their ascent.

"So tonight he dies?" the youngest pressed, leaning forward eagerly. "Tonight you kill him at his wedding feast?"

"To kill . . ." Benyamin said softly. "I want to do it, but am I able? Will I falter?"

Bracha's face came to his mind. It was the thought of his sister that hindered him. It was imagining her face when she heard the news that the brother she loved had stabbed a man to death in front of his new bride on his wedding night. She would be filled with horror and disgust. Bracha would not understand. Her womanly mind would not comprehend his defense of the law of Adonai. Her emotions should not matter. Her understanding did not affect the true and perfect law of Elohim. So why did he waver?

"Rome has ruled us long enough! We are in a war. Do we falter when it comes to the point of battle? Do your womanish doubts make the act less righteous?"

Benyamin leaned forward. This was what he needed! He needed his strength renewed, his fervor fueled.

"We are in a war, brother! We are fighting like David did the Philistines, except that the Philistines have already defeated us . . . they have already invaded us and taken us over. We are ruled by pagans and heathens. Will we sit down and accept this? Can Elohim bless us if we do?"

Excited encouraging cries rose from the men around the table, and they thumped the rough wood tabletop in agreement.

"Few men are as strong as you must be," another added. "Few men have the mind for Elohim and his law that you do. While they might worship, they do not truly enter into the mind of Elohim, because if they did, they would not be so comfortable and accepting of this wicked rule."

"Judah needs you," the oldest man added, his voice weak, but passionate. "Judah needs a man like you to do what is right even when it is hard. Judah needs a David to stand up to Goliath! Judah needs a Daniel to face a den of lions! Judah needs a warrior to defend her in the face of this brutal nation that defies the living Elohim!"

The men thumped the table and their voices rose, trying to keep their excitement as quiet as possible, but still unable to bridle their enthusiasm.

"May Adonai bless you," Benyamin said fervently. "May he keep and protect you. And may He give me the strength to do this righteous act in His holy name."

Benyamin felt his emotions as tight as a bowstring, quivering under the energy of the room. He felt it again . . . the absolute certainty. He felt it again . . . the assurance of his own righteousness. Judah needed him. He was a hero. A hero with the protection of Elohim Himself!

Later that same evening, Tzofit stood in her small room, her back to the bed she had shared with her late husband, and her face to the window. The sun had set. The sky was dusky, but not yet black with night. The moon had not yet risen to illumine a path, but the light of a few torches lightly bounced above the street. She heard the singing and talking of her approaching groom with his attendants. Their humor sounded forced. Their joy was certainly dampened. Yet they came, regardless, steadily forward. Her stomach sank as she saw them round the corner and she clearly saw the face of her groom among the taller men. He looked determined, nervous, but not glad.

She turned back to her room and looked around. Her things were packed. She wore her wedding robe, and it was beautiful—carefully embroidered and beaded. The rings her father-in-law had purchased along with the rings from her first wedding weighed heavily on her fingers. The bangles clinked softly on her wrists and the bells on her ankles tinkled out their music as she walked carefully across the room.

"Let me help you with your veil," Shahar said, pulling the veil up over her hair. She gave her daughter-in-law a smile.

"Thank you," Tzofit said. She did not know what to say. She was not moved to gush with emotion or to give a lengthy speech. She was about to be joined to a man who did not like her. She was about to be the wife of a man she could not respect. There were no words for this moment. She felt nothing but sorrow and dread.

Her husband was coming for her. She would meet him and be led through the streets to his home. There would be feasting, dancing, and singing. And then she would be taken to the bedroom where she would be considered wed.

How she would survive this evening, she did not know, but she did not have much choice. Such was the lot of a widow who needed to be provided for.

CHAPTER 23

BUT WHAT A PARTY!

As Zacchaeus looked over the dining room, he could not help but smile. Regardless of the circumstances, this was a dinner to be recorded! The finest linen tablecloths covered the tables, and flowers and sweet-scented blossoms bloomed on each one. Oil lamps scattered about the room on several different levels gave the illusion of stars sprinkled around the room. The wine was flowing freely and aroma of dishes about to be served wafted through the room like delectable fingers. Each guest's plate was unique, painted in a different floral or fauna pattern. They were a vestige of his grandfather's famous dinner parties, and now Zacchaeus had the pleasure of using them once more for this fine event. From the tasteful tapestries to the low hum of conversation, it was perfect . . . it was the dinner he had always known he could host. And the finest part of this evening was his guest of honor, the Healer who sat to his right.

Zacchaeus glanced uneasily toward his bride. Tzofit sat perfectly still at the head of the table next to him. She did not look up. Her expression was bleak but reserved. Her deep, deep unhappiness could not be hidden. She was the only mar in this perfect party, and despite his dislike of his new wife, he could not help but pity her.

"Tzofit," he said softly. "Will you have some wine?"

She did not answer him, but remained seated as she had since the evening had begun. The only sign that she had heard him was a slight compression of her lips.

Zacchaeus cleared his throat, trying to hide his embarrassment. To despise your bride was one thing. To have your bride despise you so publicly was another. At least he had the decency to hide his dislike of her in front of these people.

"It is an honor to have you attend this humble feast," Zacchaeus said, turning to Yeshua.

"I wanted to dine with you," Yeshua said. "I want to share in your celebration."

Zacchaeus' eyes flickered uncomfortably toward Tzofit, and he felt the old anger rising up inside of him.

"You had a brother," Yeshua said, tugging Zacchaeus' attention back. "He is gone now."

"How did you know?" Zacchaeus asked. He paused. "How did you know my name?"

"I know all about you," Yeshua replied. He didn't say anything more and let the silence stretch for a few moments.

"He is gone," Zacchaeus said, the old sadness coming back. "I miss him. I could use a brother on a day like this."

Yeshua put a hand on Zacchaeus' arm and they sat in silence for a few moments.

"My father was married once before he married my mother," Yeshua said after a while. "So when I was born, I already had older brothers and sisters. After me, though, my mother had eight girls."

"Eight little sisters!" Zacchaeus burst out. "Now that would be trying."

Yeshua chuckled and shook his head.

"They were great . . . really," he said. "I can still remember them running after me . . . 'Yesh, you're supposed to come home now!' 'Yesh, try the cake I made!' 'Yesh, carry me to that tree!'"

Zacchaeus shared a knowing look with Yeshua. Siblings were like that. They might irritate you, drive you mad, but you could never get them out of your blood.

"You must wish your brother were with you today to celebrate," Yeshua said.

Zacchaeus frowned despite himself. "You should know that this marriage is not exactly a celebration," he said with a low voice. "You might have noticed our dislike for each other. She is my brother's widow. I wish he were here, yes, but also that I were marrying a different woman."

Yeshua nodded. "Let me tell you a story . . . There once was a shepherd with a flock of sheep. One day a little lamb went missing. He searched for it everywhere, leaving the rest of the flock with his brothers. He searched all day, and when night came he heard a faint baa in a thicket. He bent down and pulled the hungry little lamb out of the thorns and brought it back to the camp. Don't you think that he would have celebrated upon finding that sheep?"

"Of course," Zacchaeus said, shaking his head. "But how is this a celebration for a lost sheep?"

"Your family had the care of this woman," Yeshua said quietly. "She is now hungry and worn. You have found her, and while you do not realize it now, you will find later on that today was indeed reason to celebrate. Trust in Elohim."

Zacchaeus felt a lump rise in his throat and his eyes misted with tears. Could Elohim make this mess right again? Could Elohim straighten out a life as damaged and lonely as his? Would He?

The bangles and rings on Tzofit's hands seemed to weigh more than a water jug, and lifting her hands was more effort than she cared to expend. She looked down at the food piled on the plate before her with no desire to taste it. It was exquisite. The dinner was exceptional. The décor, the food, the entertainment . . . all was more than she'd ever expected, yet she could find no amount of joy inside of her.

Glancing over at her new husband, she looked down at him, trying to hide her distain. His head barely came past her shoulder, and he was deep in conversation with the healer, Yeshua. How Zacchaeus had snared such a distinguished guest, she had no idea, but the man was here. She felt a slow wave of despair descend upon her.

She looked down at her hands with the sparkling rings and the bangles around her wrists, and she thought, *This is the day of my second marriage.* She would remember this day. All women remembered the day of their marriage, but her memories would never be happy ones. She knew it. This was the beginning of the rest of her life.

"I will survive this," Tzofit whispered to herself. "I will."

"Pardon me?" a servant asked. "Did you ask for something?"

"No," she said. "I asked for nothing."

She would never ask for anything. She would avoid her husband as much as possible, beginning tonight. But how? How did a wife, who was bound to a man to serve him and give him children, manage to avoid him? How could she live separately from him in the same house, when she must prepare his food and sleep in his bed?

"Tzofit," Zacchaeus murmured, leaning closer. "Could you try to look less dismal?"

"It is unlikely," she whispered back, repressed anger quivering in her voice.

He gave her an unreadable look and retreated to his food, focusing on the plate as if it were a battle to be fought. And he would have a battle to fight, she realized with a small amount of satisfaction. She had no intention of making this marriage easy on Zacchaeus. None at all.

Ehud stared at the food on the table before him. There was a central platter of meat from a fattened calf, a large dish of stewed vegetables, and several smaller platters of goat's cheese and barley rolled in pickled grape leaves mingled with other delicacies. It was a meal he should be relishing . . . a meal the likes he would never encounter again. But his mind was not on the food, or on the excellent wine. In fact, it all tasted like sand on his tongue, and he struggled to swallow out of politeness to his host. Ehud's mind was on his daughter, and each time he saw a servant moving silently and quickly through the room, he wondered whose child she was, and if her father was thinking of her, too.

He had not wanted to come to this wedding celebration for the food and the company. He had come for a reason—to beg Zacchaeus to help him save his daughter. It was not an appropriate time, but he could not wait any longer. He had tried to see Zacchaeus before the wedding, but he had not been successful. But he must succeed! If he did not get an answer from the wealthy tax collector, he felt like he would die.

Elohim, grant me mercy tonight! he prayed silently. *Let this man help me. And while I am not able, protect my little girl . . .*

What was happening to her, he did not know. Nor did he want to think. His eyes were on the host and groom of this wedding dinner, watching in agonized impatience as the little man chatted with the honored guest, Yeshua, and made merry with the others.

Ehud had been waiting all evening for a chance to speak to Zacchaeus, and had almost despaired that his opportunity would come, when Zacchaeus suddenly excused himself. Ehud slipped from his place at the table and followed several steps behind the groom and out of the house. Ehud called out.

"Sir?"

Zacchaeus turned, frowning.

"Who is there?" he asked.

"It is I, sir," Ehud said, coming out into the light. "I must speak with you."

"Now?" Zacchaeus sighed. "I am not concerning myself with

business tonight, my friend. I will hear what you have to tell me after my honeymoon."

"Please."

There must have been something in Ehud's voice that rang of sincerity, because Zacchaeus stopped and looked at the man who regularly reported to him.

"What is it, then?" Zacchaeus asked. "We do not have much time."

"I don't know how to begin," Ehud said, the words coming out in a rush. "I am in debt. Terrible debt. I made some foolish decisions and borrowed a large amount of money. I am unable to repay it, sir."

"And you want more work from me?" Zacchaeus asked.

"No, sir," Ehud said. "It is more desperate than that. The money lender has taken my daughter into slavery in exchange for my debt."

"And?" Zacchaeus asked.

"Sir, I am desperate to get her back. She is only 11. Young, obedient, pretty. She is a good girl, and she does not deserve this."

"No, she does not," Zacchaeus said frankly. "But you must have known the risks when you got yourself into debt!"

"I was as stupid as a yearling lamb," Ehud said. "But my daughter . . ."

"And you want my help?" Zacchaeus asked reluctantly.

"Yes."

"How?"

"I beg you to pay my debt, sir," Ehud said. "And in return, I will give myself to you in slavery."

Zacchaeus looked up at Ehud in silence for several moments. He frowned, then suddenly shook his head and threw his hands in the air.

"You come to me on my wedding day?" he demanded in anger. "Today? When I am hosting a wedding dinner! You come now?"

"Sir, I could not wait!"

"I am not in a position to discuss your massive debts," Zacchaeus retorted. "I am expected back in that dining room any minute now. You come to me now? No! No! I will not listen to you about this. You have done something foolish, and you are reaping the consequences! Do not make your misery mine, especially on this day."

Ehud watched silently as Zacchaeus walked briskly away from him, muttering in disgust under his breath.

"My wife offers herself, too," Ehud whispered impotently.

The only hope he knew of for his daughter's freedom had just turned his back on him.

CHAPTER 24

Ͳʜᴇ Wᴇᴅᴅɪɴɢ Nɪɢʜͳ

Back inside the house, Zacchaeus stole a glance in the direction of Tzofit. Her large eyes fringed with thick lashes were downcast and she seemed to be lost in thought. The jeweled chain sparkled across her forehead, and the embroidered veil lay against her smooth cheek, her hair perfectly hidden from sight. She was beautiful, this angry, sullen wife of his.

Ehud's words kept running through his mind, however. His daughter was enslaved, and the man would offer himself in her place. Zacchaeus wondered if his father would have done the same for him. For Oshri, yes. Oshri was his father's joy, and his imprint. He was just like his father. Zacchaeus was not. He was nothing like his father, and he was bred in sin. It's what the city had said about him. They'd called him a runt, a dwarf, a curse from above. They'd said that his filth could rub off on their fingers if they touched him. They said that any man's daughter who was given to him in marriage would be cursed to bear children as hideous as he was. He had been excluded. He had been hated. He had been shunned. And right now, he honestly doubted that his father loved him the way Ehud loved his little daughter.

"You look thoughtful," Yeshua said, and Zacchaeus started out of his reverie.

"It is a big day," Zacchaeus said. "I have much to think about."

Yeshua nodded.

"When women are about to marry, their mothers give them advice," Yeshua said quietly.

Zacchaeus frowned.

"What sort?" he asked.

"They tell them that a good wife is not good because she has a good husband. She is good because she performs her duties well and she fills her role admirably. A woman can be a good wife despite the sort of husband she is given to," Yeshua said. "I know this because my mother gave similar advice to my younger sisters."

Zacchaeus sighed and looked down at the food before him.

"The same can be said for sons," Yeshua said. "Or men. We are who we are because of how we act, my friend. Our birth, our parents, our situations do not need to rule us."

"Our deformities?" Zacchaeus asked.

"They give us more opportunity to develop our characters," Yeshua said. "Do you like who you are, Zacchaeus?"

"Do I like who I am?" Zacchaeus repeated. "No, I don't! I don't like my ridiculously short height. I don't like my position in society. I don't like a great many things."

"But do you like who you *are*?" Yeshua repeated. "Do you like the man you have become?"

Zacchaeus was silent. No, he did not. He did not like his anger. He did not like his hardness. There were too many things he did not like about the man he had become. Too many things he did not like to think of.

"There is a story about a man who owed a great deal of money," Yeshua said. As he spoke the table grew quiet, and attention turned toward the Healer. "In fact, it was money his dead father had owed, and the debt had been passed on to him. He struggled to pay, but could not. So he went to the man who had lent the money to his father, and he said, 'Sir, I have tried and tried to repay you, but I cannot. It is beyond my ability. Please, have mercy on me. Give me a little more time, and I will find a way.' The wealthy man considered. He knew that he could have the man imprisoned and enslave his family as recompense, but he did not want to do that. He said, 'I forgive your debt.'"

There was a murmur of surprise around the table.

"Forgiven?" somebody said. "Who would do that?"

"The story goes on," Yeshua said, holding up one hand. "The man who was forgiven the unpayable debt, was walking home to tell his family of the good news. On his way, he came upon a man who owed him a small pittance . . . enough to buy lunch from a stall at the market. 'Repay me what you owe!' he said. 'Please,' the man replied. 'I do not have the money, but if you will be merciful to me, I will pay you back in full.'"

Yeshua was silent.

"What happened?" someone asked.

"He had the man beaten and threatened to have him thrown in prison if he did not repay," Yeshua replied simply.

"Horrible!" Zacchaeus said. "After all he had been forgiven!"

"Who had the bigger debt?" Yeshua asked. "Yet who was more judgmental?"

The room was silent. Zacchaeus looked down at his hands. His mind was spinning and as he looked up, he saw Yeshua looking at him with an expression of understanding.

"Master," Zacchaeus said, standing to his feet and putting his hands together in a sign of respect. "I don't like who I am. I want to be a different man. Today, in fact, this very minute, I give half of my wealth to pay the debt of a certain poor man here in Yericho who has asked me for help." Zacchaeus looked in the direction of Ehud, meeting his surprised gaze for a brief moment before looking away in embarrassment. "And if anyone here believes I am a crook, if I have ever cheated anyone in my position of tax collector, or even in my personal life, I will make restitution. I will give back four times what I have taken!"

After a shocked silence whispers rippled around the room.

"My friend, Zacchaeus," Yeshua said with a broad smile. "I say this today in the presence of all here: you are truly a Judean in high standing, my friend, no matter what marketplace gossip might say! The Son of Man came searching to find and restore those who have lost their way. You are back on track."

Zaccheaus stood awkwardly for a moment longer, then moved away from the table, eager to be away from the stares and whispers. He stood at the side of the room, looking back at the table where Yeshua was saying something to his bride, his hands put together in front of him in respect.

"Thank you!" Ehud whispered, and Zacchaeus turned in surprise to see the man at his side, tears filling his eyes. "Allow me to fetch my daughter, and I will be yours as a slave."

"No, no!" Zacchaeus said. "You will keep your freedom, Ehud."

Before Ehud could reply, the music struck up, and the table began to clap in time to the traditional wedding dance. Pushing themselves to their feet and catching the rhythm in their movements, the men let out a whoop of celebration. Some women came in and pulled at Tzofit, tugging her into a circle of laughter and singing, and Zacchaeus took the hand of the man offering it, the music tugging him into the rhythm of the traditional dance. He looked in surprise into the face of Yeshua.

"You are married, my friend!" Yeshua laughed. "Dance! A wife is a blessing from Adonai!"

That night, in his own home, Zacchaeus stood in his bedroom, his new bride standing awkwardly to one side. The room was dim and some refreshments had been laid out in preparation for their evening together. She was as still as a statue, her eyes flickering from one spot to another on the floor in front of her.

"Tzofit," he said softly.

She was silent.

"I will not touch you tonight."

She was still silent, but a tear slid down her cheek and her chest began to move in quick breaths as she tried to control her emotion. He spread his hands in defeat, giving his new wife a sheepish smile.

"I did not choose to make you miserable, Tzofit," he said. "The family chose for me. But I will do my best to be kind to you."

"You hate me," she said, her voice quivering. "As much as I hate you."

"There you are wrong," he replied, shaking his head. "I'm terrified of you, though."

She laughed at this through her tears, wiping at her face.

Zacchaeus was silent for a moment, then he laughed quietly to himself and shrugged.

"Sleep well, my wife," he said, turning to leave the room, but he stopped as he reached the door. He turned back to see her watching him in confusion.

"It is not right to join with you while you hate me," he said, shaking his head. "But perhaps tomorrow you would be willing to sit with me while we eat fine honeymoon foods . . . just sit and talk."

"You would consent to that?" she whispered.

"It is a strange desire of mine," he said quietly, "to have a companion I could talk to . . . and who might enjoy a fine meal."

With that, he turned and left the room to spend the night of his wedding alone.

Benyamin took a deep breath, willing his body to melt into the darkness of the night. The hum of voices was coming from inside the house, laughter and conversation rolling out in the street in waves. The street was quiet, except for the merriment of the wedding within the house, and he watched while a squadron of Roman soldiers marched past, eyeing him suspiciously, then moving on with the stamp of their feet and the clatter of their armor. He licked his lips and raised his eyes to the starry sky, slightly obliterated by the haze of dust and cooking fires.

"Adonai, grant me success," he whispered. "This is for your glory!"

Looking around himself cautiously, Benyamin slipped around the house, keeping his body close to the sandblasted walls. He slid his blade from its sheath, scraping his thumb against the blade to check for its sharpness. He smiled in satisfaction.

Benyamin came to a window lit from within. He peeked around the side and saw a woman standing alone. She wore her wedding garments and her arms were wrapped around her waist as if she could hold her body together with her own grasp. Tears were trickling down her cheeks and she sobbed quietly, her mouth open and her breath coming in shuddering gasps.

The bride. He watched her in surprise. Her husband was not with her, however, and he moved on past the window, his feet crunching quietly against the rocky ground. He heard a noise, and he froze, looking quickly behind him. It was nothing. He exhaled in relief, then continued his way around the house. Another window was coming up, and it too was lit from within.

"It is a fine evening."

Benyamin jumped, whirling around with his knife raised in defense. His eyes snapped around, looking for the one who spoke. A man stood in front of him, his head uncovered and a smile playing at his lips. He was tall, well muscled and solid, but he did not look threatening. Benyamin looked quickly at his knife and put it away, shaking his head.

"I apologize, sir," Benyamin said. "You alarmed me."

"Out for a walk?" the man asked.

"Yes, yes," Benyamin said quickly. "I was clearing my head."

"Your head could use some clearing," the man said, his eyes catching Benyamin's. "Murder will not make you more righteous, my friend."

"Murder?" Benyamin laughed. "I would not have killed you, sir!"

"But you would kill Zacchaeus?" he asked.

"Who are you?" Benyamin demanded.

"A guest," the man replied.

Benyamin looked closer, frowning.

"You are that healer they speak of," he said suddenly. "The one they say is the Messiah!"

"It is what they say." Yeshua replied.

"You don't look very kingly to me," Benyamin said. "You look more like a common laborer!"

"If I were a common laborer," Yeshua said. "Would I be less righteous?"

Benyamin was silent.

"You love the law of my Father," Yeshua said quietly. "You would die to protect it!"

"I would kill to protect it," Benyamin whispered. "Israel has fallen away from Adonai. We are held by the Romans as a punishment for our own sin. Who is left who is righteous? Who is left who will stand for the Law?"

"The Law is certainly righteous," Yeshua agreed. "The Law points to the most righteous one of all . . . the Messiah. Every act, every requirement is an arrow pointing the way to the One who will save Israel. But you, my friend, are not righteous."

Benyamin scowled then spat on the ground.

"Do you care about Israel?" Benyamin retorted. "Do you care that our nation has been raped by these pigs? Do you care that Adonai has turned His face from His people because of their stinking sins? Do you care about our pride? Do you care about the Law of Adonai, the one perfect command that has been trampled for generations? Do you care about any of it?"

Yeshua was silent.

"I care!" Benyamin went on. "I care about Isreal's pride, her purity and her righteousness. *I* care!"

Yeshua nodded.

"You do," he said. "I believe you, Benyamin."

At the sound of his name, Benyamin looked up in surprise.

"You care a great deal, my friend," Yeshua said. "My Father longs for these things as well. But there is something of more importance to Adonai than even the defense of His Law."

"Which is?"

"You."

Benyamin blinked. He swallowed and shook his head.

"No, you are mistaken," Benyamin said. "There are things of much more importance than one man. We battle together for the bigger cause."

"Why has the Messiah come?" Yeshua asked.

"To save Israel from Rome, of course!"

"The Messiah came because He knew that there would be a baby boy born one morning," Yeshua said. "His father would be poor and his closest friend would be his younger sister. He would hate the poverty that encrusted him. He would hate the wickedness he saw around him, and one day as a young man, he would be lured into a secret association with men who would use him. That young man would be convinced that he was acting by the will of Adonai, but really he would be acting out of a desperate hope that this was not all there was to life. He would be willing to kill in order to prove to himself that he was more than a poor boy, covered in dust and kicked around by everyone from his father to the wealthy men who hired him as a day laborer."

"The Messiah came for a poor boy?" Benyamin asked with a weak laugh.

"That poor boy was created for a purpose," Yeshua replied. "Adonai formed him in his mother's womb, and He gave that boy a passion for His Law. He gave him a stubbornness of heart and a desire for more than the gutters of Yericho. Adonai created that boy, lovingly formed him, and breathed life into his tiny form."

"A purpose?" Benyamin whispered.

"A purpose," Yeshua replied with a nod. "But your purpose, Benyamin, is not to take life. Your purpose is to look at the Law given by My Father and see Who it pointed to."

"Are you the Messiah?" Benyamin asked.

"Appearances can be deceiving, can't they?" Yeshua asked. "Look to the Law and the Prophets, Benyamin, and remember that appearances can be deceiving."

"And what of Israel?" Benyamin asked.

"What of it?" Yeshua said quietly.

Benyamin was silent.

"Leave Israel to My Father," Yeshua said. "The Messiah came for you, a poor boy who was tired of being kicked around like garbage. The Messiah came for Zacchaeus, a tax collector who was tired of being rejected and thought that some coins would fill his heart."

"Zacchaeus?" Benyamin spat out.

"Do you know what matters more to my Father than His Law?" Yeshua asked.

Benyamin was silent.

"A man's heart."

As Yeshua walked away, back toward the party and the laughter, Benyamin stood in the darkness, a light beginning to shine in his mind like the pinpricks of starlight.

"Do I matter to You, oh Adonai?" Benyamin silently prayed.

Yeshua stopped in his steps, turned around, and let out a laugh that echoed against the stone walls of Yericho's houses.

"Yes!" Yeshua called out. "A hundred times, Yes!"

CHAPTER 25

FAREWELL

Gaius Markus Africanus looked down at the neat little scroll Zacchaeus had put in his hand. He looked back up at the little tax collector with his neatly trimmed beard and his excellently cut robe. Zacchaeus rubbed his hands together.

"Then it is done," he said.

"You are sure you want to leave your post as tax collector?" Gaius asked. "The payment is no incentive to you?"

"I am sure," Zacchaeus said. "We Jews have a saying, that we are pressed but not crushed, persecuted but not forsaken."

"And Rome is the oppression?" Gauis asked with a chuckle.

"The oppression came long before Rome," Zacchaeus replied. "But I must do what I must do. I will miss you, Gaius."

Gaius nodded, feeling the awkwardness of a goodbye he hadn't realized would touch him so much. "It is just as well," he said. "I am being transferred."

"Really?" Zacchaeus asked. "Where?"

"Jerusalem," Gaius said. "Execution duty. Golgotha."

They were both silent.

"It's not pleasant," Gaius said by way of apology. "But it's justice."

"With no mercy."

"No," Gaius agreed. "No mercy."

"I will miss our business together," Zacchaeus said.

Gaius gave a curt nod.

"You are fortunate, friend," Gaius said suddenly.

"Am I?" Zacchaeus asked.

"A Jew has a God to make peace with," Gaius said. "A Roman does not make peace with his gods. He does his duty to them, and then he makes peace with himself."

Zacchaeus nodded slowly, his eyes meeting Gaius' in a sad look.

"I suspect that your God is more forgiving than I am," Gaius said quietly. "May whatever God you worship sustain you."

"And you," Zacchaeus replied quietly. "And you."

So as Gaius oversaw the taxes being loaded into the chariot, and he glanced back at the house and the odd little man who stood looking out into the street. Zacchaeus was different now after his marriage. They said that marriage changed a man, but this was something more. The man had lost his desperate, needy look. He had changed into a more confident, quieter man. Gaius did not understand it. But he did not have time to puzzle out the life of a Judean tax collector. He had a life of his own . . . a life that was facing changes, too.

What would Jerusalem hold for a centurion stationed at Golgotha? Gaius did not know. But he hoped, in some way, to find some peace.

Epilogue

Time had passed. Days had melted into months, and months into seasons. The season had changed and the rains had come, pouring water onto the earth and buffeting the trees with wind that drove rain against the withered, thirsty leaves. Houses were closed up tight, leather covers dropped over windows, and doors slammed shut. Lazy fingers of smoke from cooking fires meandered up into the air, trapped in a moist layer over the city of Yericho.

In a beautiful house, near the center of the city, Zacchaeus sat indoors, listening to the sound of the rain pounding against the street outside. Distantly, the rumble of thunder echoed, but just outside, under a covered area of the courtyard, he could hear his wife humming as she cooked. He had tried hinting that they could afford to have servants cook for them, but she wouldn't hear of it—unfortunately. She was the woman of this house, and she would cook. Tzofit was a force to be reckoned with.

"Tzofit," he called, raising his voice so she could hear him.

She made a sound that said that she heard him.

"I saw the most beautiful veil that I wanted to buy for you," he called. "It was Egyptian cotton and as soft as silk. You would have loved it."

"Hmm?" her voice came from the courtyard.

"I wanted to reach it, but it was put too high. I was too embarrassed to ask the merchant to reach it for me. I'll go back for it tomorrow if it is still there," he said, then added with a chuckle, "I'm a wealthy man with a beautiful wife. All I lack is two feet of height!"

Tzofit pushed back the curtain that separated the courtyard from the rest of the house and reemerged, belly first. It still amazed him to see the change in her body with her pregnancy. She walked differently, awkwardly, beautifully.

"Husband," she said, frowning in thought and looking at Zacchaeus' shoes as she spoke. "There are many kinds of men in the world. Some men are small in their minds and never grow past their mother's skirts. Some men are small in stature, or in the public eyes. But you, Zacchaeus . . . to me . . ." She stammered and stopped, embarrassed.

Zacchaeus looked at her, watching her as she smoothed her hand over her belly.

". . . you, husband," she said, "are a strong man . . . a good man."

Tzofit lifted her eyes to look quickly at her husband, gauging his reaction, watching for laughter.

"You are big," she whispered, "in my eyes."

And with that, she turned and left the room, disappearing behind the curtain once more. Zacchaeus stared after her, tears misting his eyes.

For the first time in his life, he realized what it felt like to be loved by a woman.

He straightened his shoulders. In his heart, he had just gained two feet of height.